Pokémon Adventures™

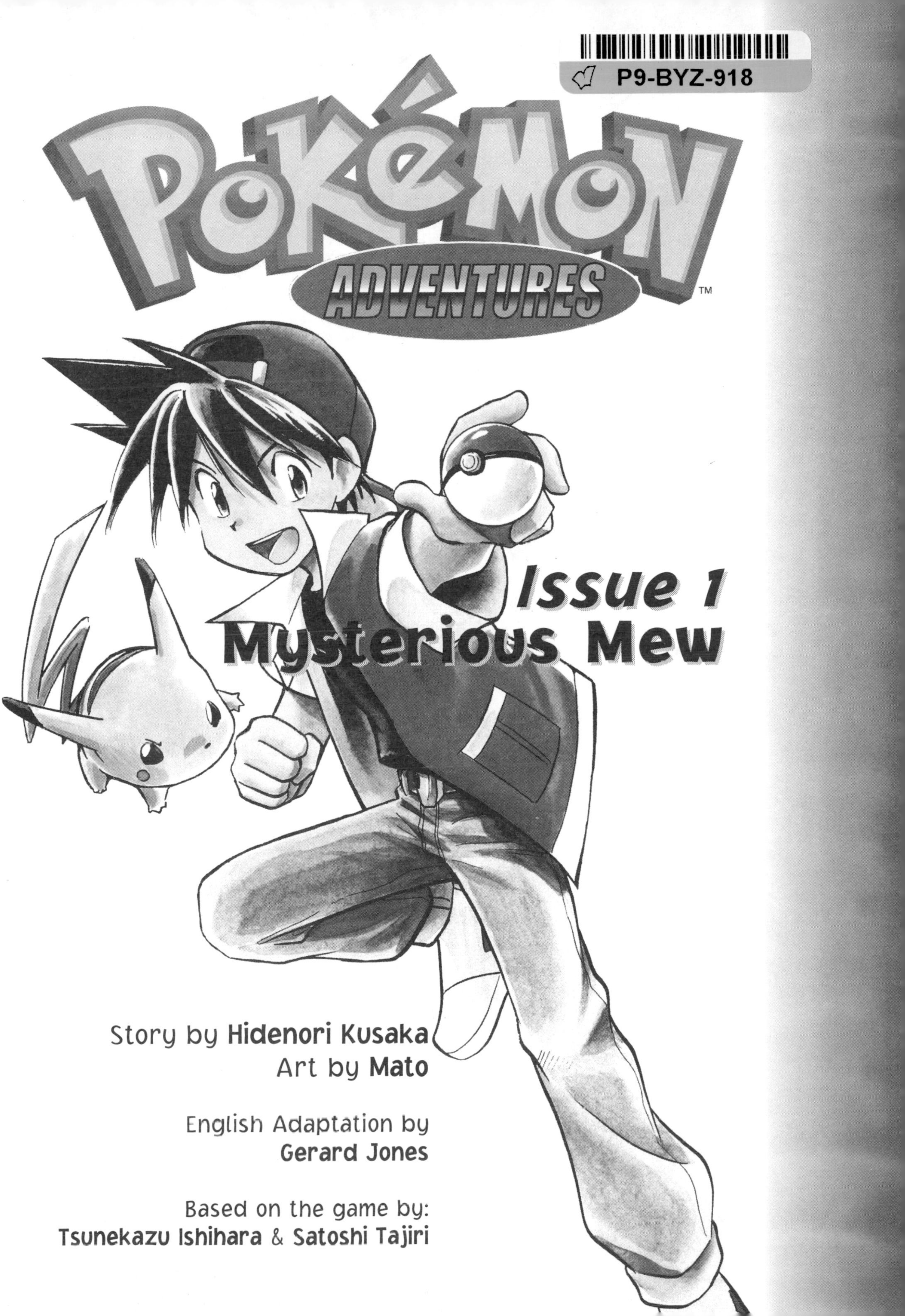

Issue 1
Mysterious Mew

Story by **Hidenori Kusaka**
Art by **Mato**

English Adaptation by
Gerard Jones

Based on the game by:
Tsunekazu Ishihara & **Satoshi Tajiri**

POKéMON ADVENTURES
Issue 1:
Mysterious Mew

Story/Hidenori Kusaka
Art/Mato

English Adaptation/Gerard Jones

Translation/Kaori Inoue
Touch-up & Lettering/Dan Nakrosis
Graphics & Design/Carolina Ugalde
Editing/William Flanagan

Editor-in-Chief/Hyoe Narita
Publisher/Seiji Horibuchi

First published by
Shogakukan, Inc. in Japan.

© 1995, 1996 and 1998 Nintendo,
CREATURES, GAME FREAK.
™ & ® are trademarks of Nintendo.
© 1999 Nintendo.

The stories, characters and incidents
mentioned in this publication are
entirely fictional. For the purposes of
publication in English, the artwork in
this publication is in reverse from
the original Japanese version.
Printed in Canada.
First printing, September 1999.

Published by Viz Comics
P.O. Box 77064
San Francisco, CA 94107

For advertising opportunities, call:
Oliver Chin
Director of Sales and Marketing
(415) 546-7073 ext. 128

Ask for our **free**
Viz Shop-By-Mail catalog!

Call toll free: (800) 394-3042
Or visit us on-line at our web site:
www.viz.com. And check out our
internet magazines: j-pop.com at
www.j-pop.com and Animerica at
www.animerica-mag! Get your
free Viz newsletter at j-pop.com!

CONTENTS

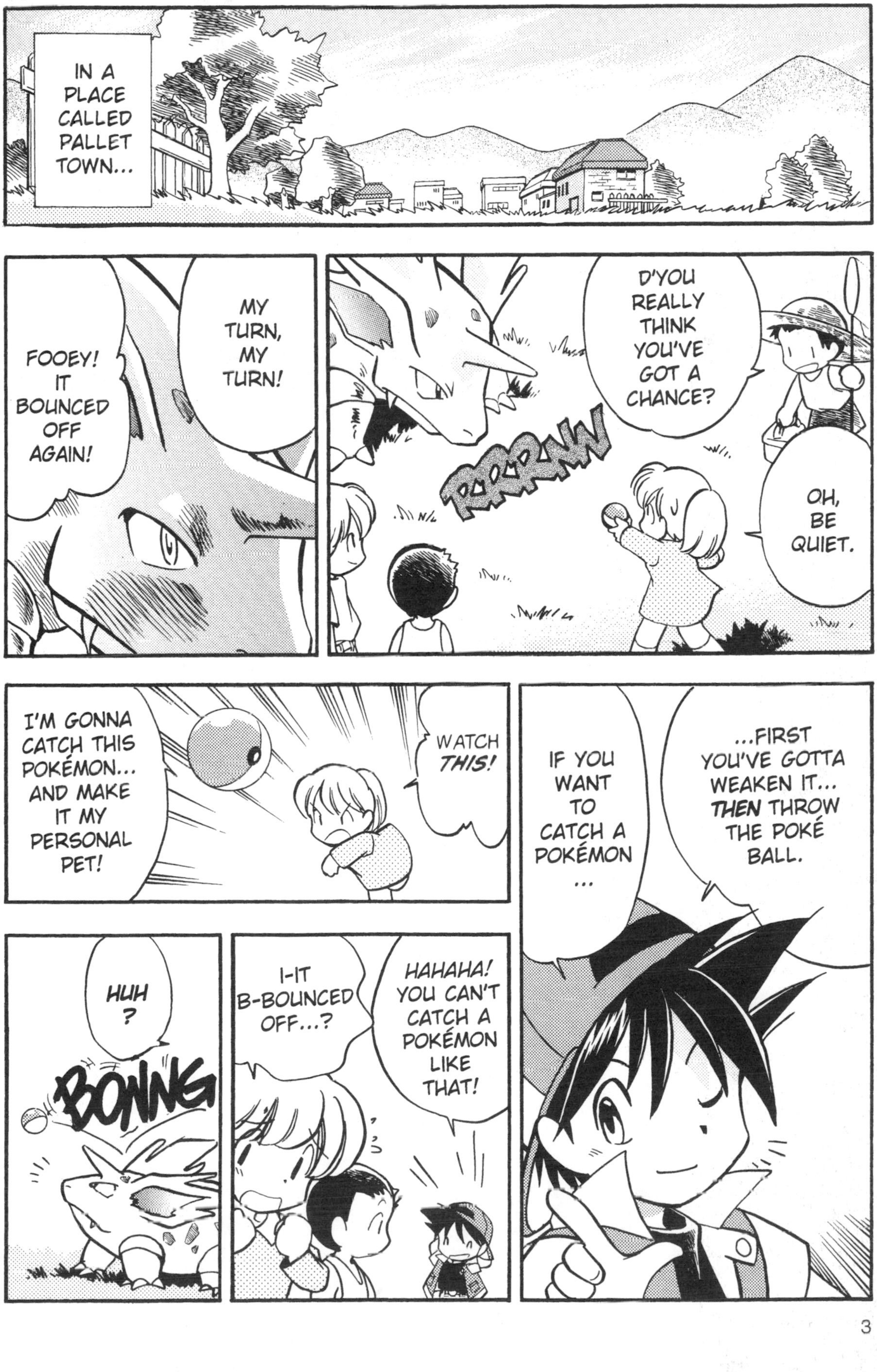
IN A PLACE CALLED PALLET TOWN...
FOOEY! IT BOUNCED OFF AGAIN!
MY TURN, MY TURN!
D'YOU REALLY THINK YOU'VE GOT A CHANCE?
ROOARNW
OH, BE QUIET.
I'M GONNA CATCH THIS POKÉMON... AND MAKE IT MY PERSONAL PET!
WATCH *THIS!*
HUH ?
BONNG
I-IT B-BOUNCED OFF...?
HAHAHA! YOU CAN'T CATCH A POKÉMON LIKE THAT!
IF YOU WANT TO CATCH A POKÉMON ...
...FIRST YOU'VE GOTTA WEAKEN IT... **THEN** THROW THE POKÉ BALL.

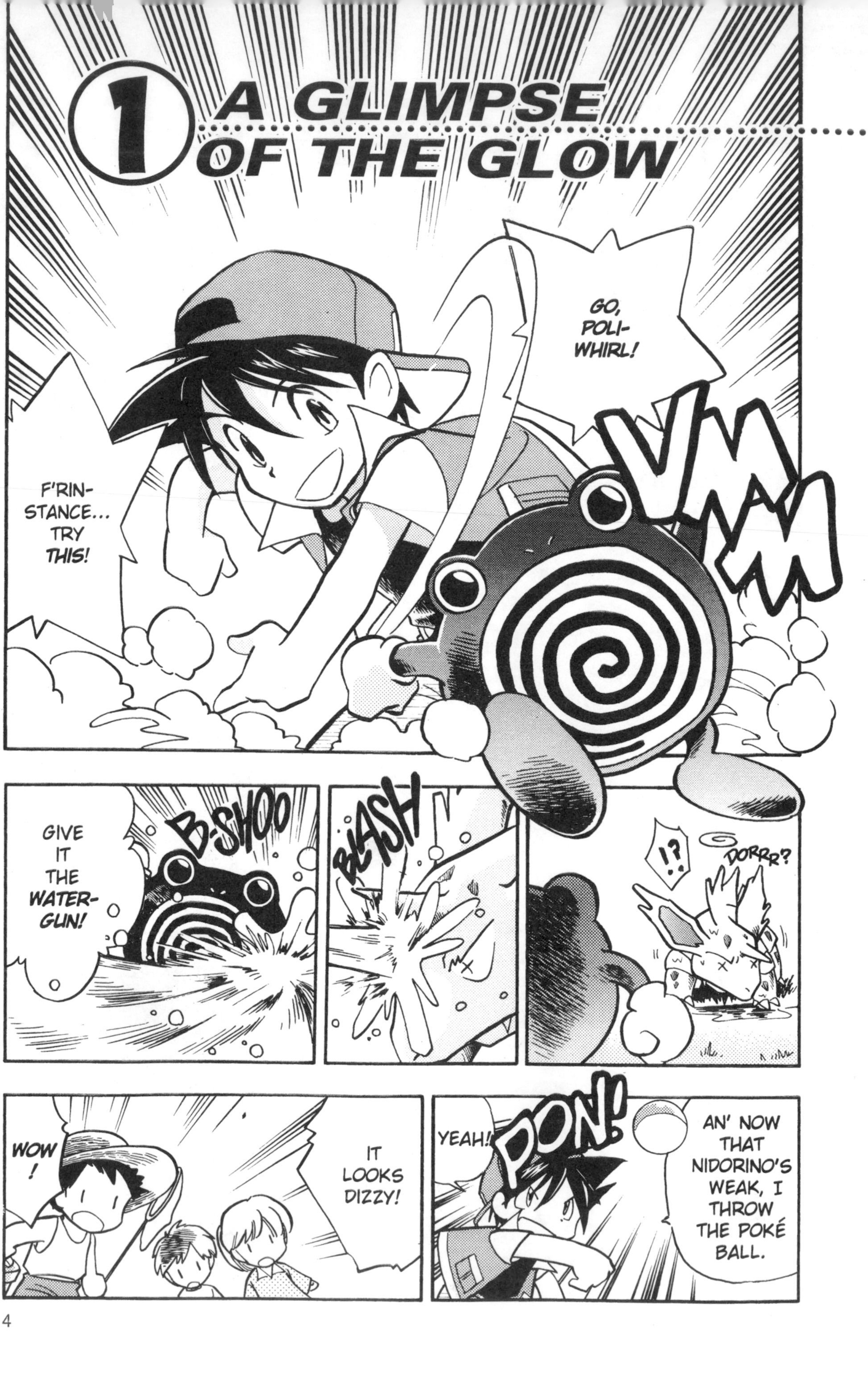
1 A GLIMPSE OF THE GLOW
GO, POLI-WHIRL!
F'RIN-STANCE... TRY THIS!
VMMM
GIVE IT THE WATER-GUN!
B-SHOO
BLASH
!?
DORRR?
WOW!
IT LOOKS DIZZY!
YEAH!
PON!
AN' NOW THAT NIDORINO'S WEAK, I THROW THE POKÉ BALL.

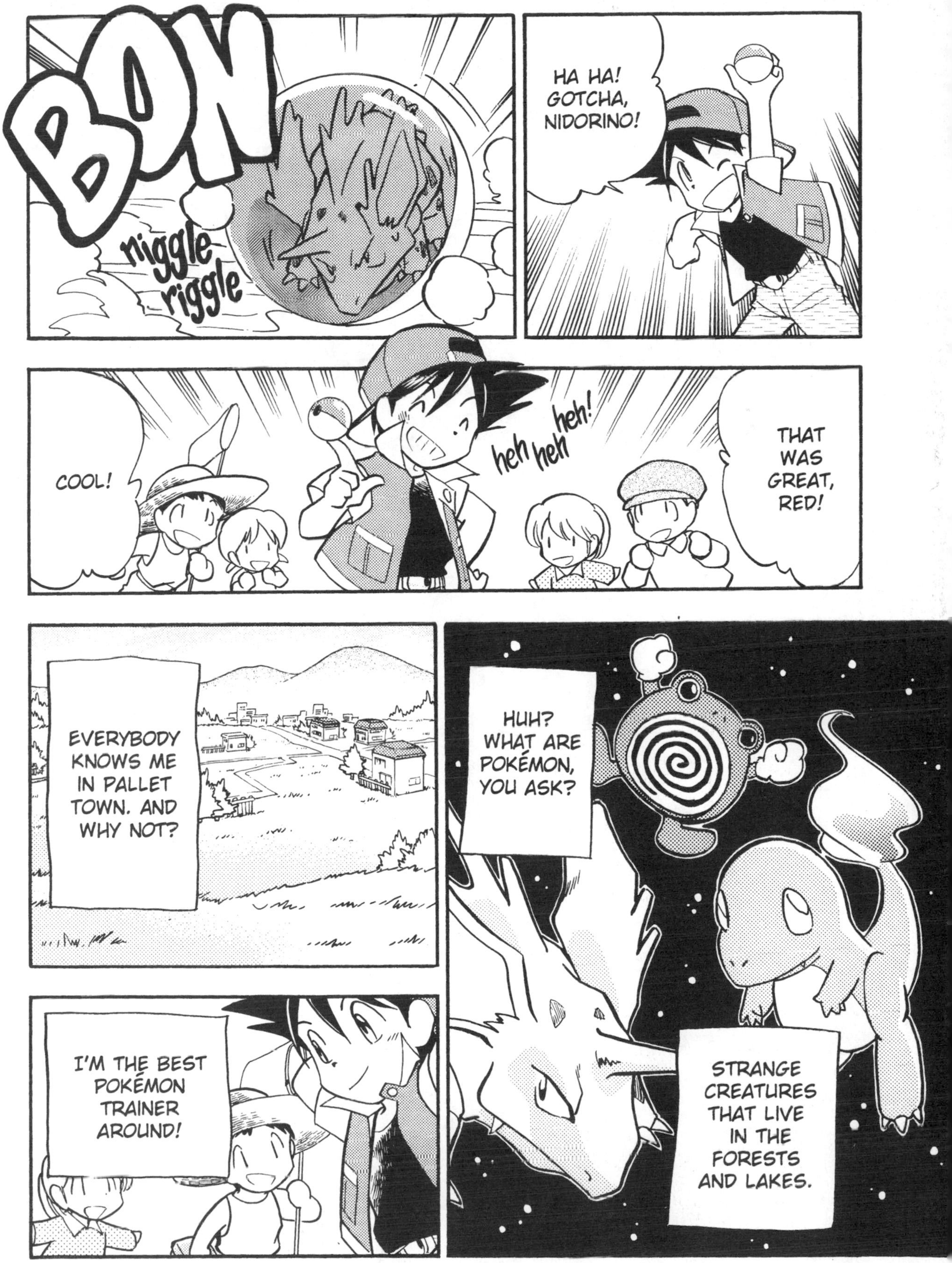
BON
riggle riggle
HA HA! GOTCHA, NIDORINO!
COOL!
heh heh heh!
THAT WAS GREAT, RED!
EVERYBODY KNOWS ME IN PALLET TOWN. AND WHY NOT?
I'M THE BEST POKÉMON TRAINER AROUND!
HUH? WHAT ARE POKÉMON, YOU ASK?
STRANGE CREATURES THAT LIVE IN THE FORESTS AND LAKES.

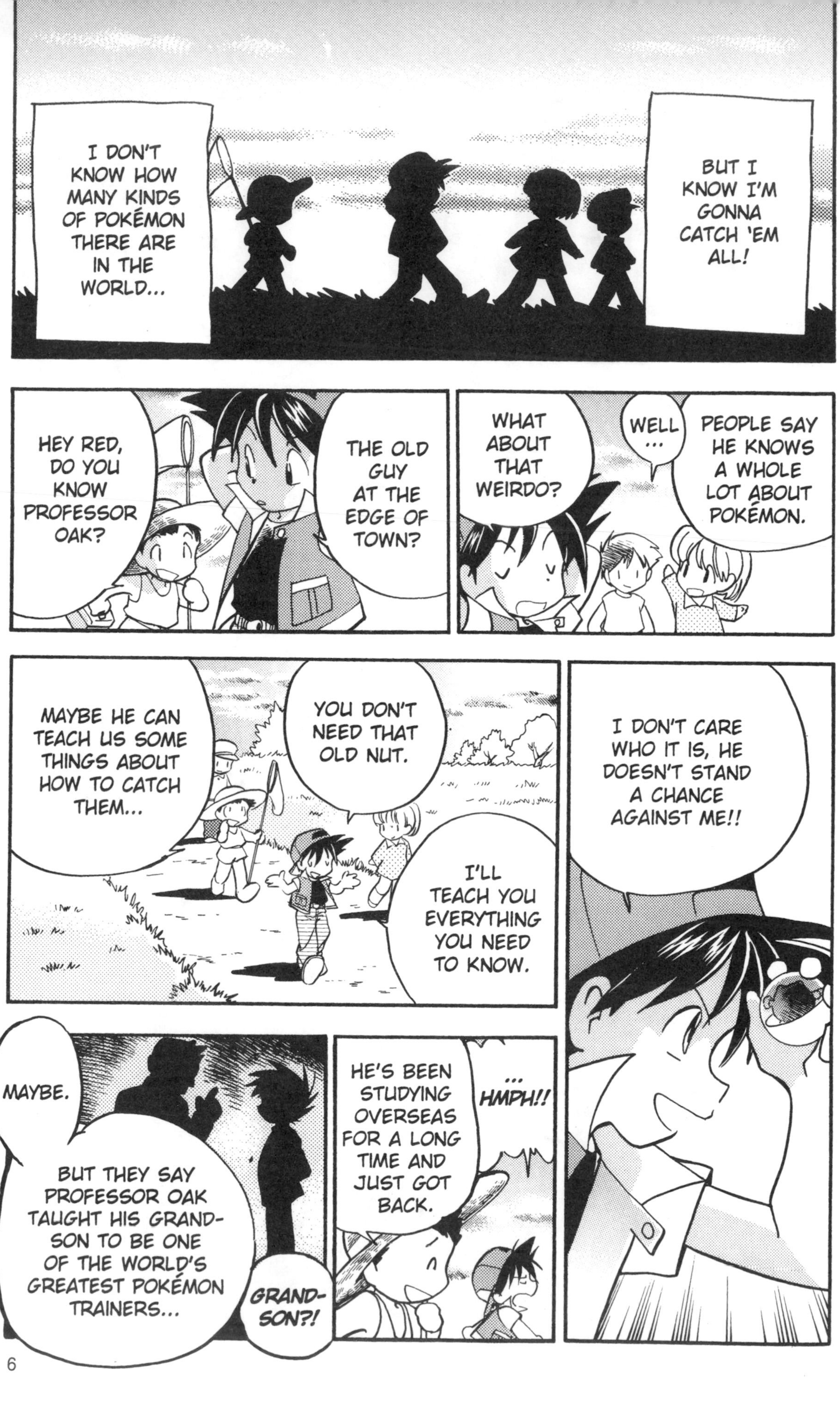
I DON'T KNOW HOW MANY KINDS OF POKÉMON THERE ARE IN THE WORLD...
BUT I KNOW I'M GONNA CATCH 'EM ALL!
HEY RED, DO YOU KNOW PROFESSOR OAK?
THE OLD GUY AT THE EDGE OF TOWN?
WHAT ABOUT THAT WEIRDO?
WELL...
PEOPLE SAY HE KNOWS A WHOLE LOT ABOUT POKÉMON.
MAYBE HE CAN TEACH US SOME THINGS ABOUT HOW TO CATCH THEM...
YOU DON'T NEED THAT OLD NUT.
I'LL TEACH YOU EVERYTHING YOU NEED TO KNOW.
I DON'T CARE WHO IT IS, HE DOESN'T STAND A CHANCE AGAINST ME!!
MAYBE.
BUT THEY SAY PROFESSOR OAK TAUGHT HIS GRAND-SON TO BE ONE OF THE WORLD'S GREATEST POKÉMON TRAINERS...
GRAND-SON?!
HE'S BEEN STUDYING OVERSEAS FOR A LONG TIME AND JUST GOT BACK.
... HMPH!!

SEE YOU TO-MORROW!

SEE YA!

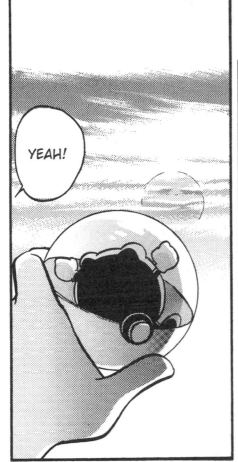

YEAH!

HMM...

OLD PRO-FESSOR OAK, HUH...?

OOMF!

VOMP

HEY!

WATCH IT, YOU WORM!

EEP!

WH-WHERE'D THOSE GUYS COME FROM?

TROMP! TROMP!

HEY!

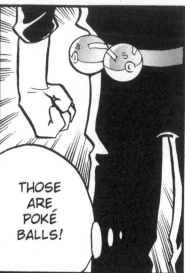

THOSE ARE POKÉ BALLS!

THEY'VE GOTTA BE POKÉMON TRAINERS.

KSH KSH KSH KSH

IT MUST BE HIDING IN THIS GENERAL AREA!!

DO NOT REST UNTIL YOU FIND IT!

FIND THE PHANTOM POKÉMON!!

PHAN-TOM POKÉ-MON?

NEVER HEARD OF IT!

WE HAVE NOT YET SEARCHED THE WEST WOOD!

COMB IT TO THE LAST BLADE!!

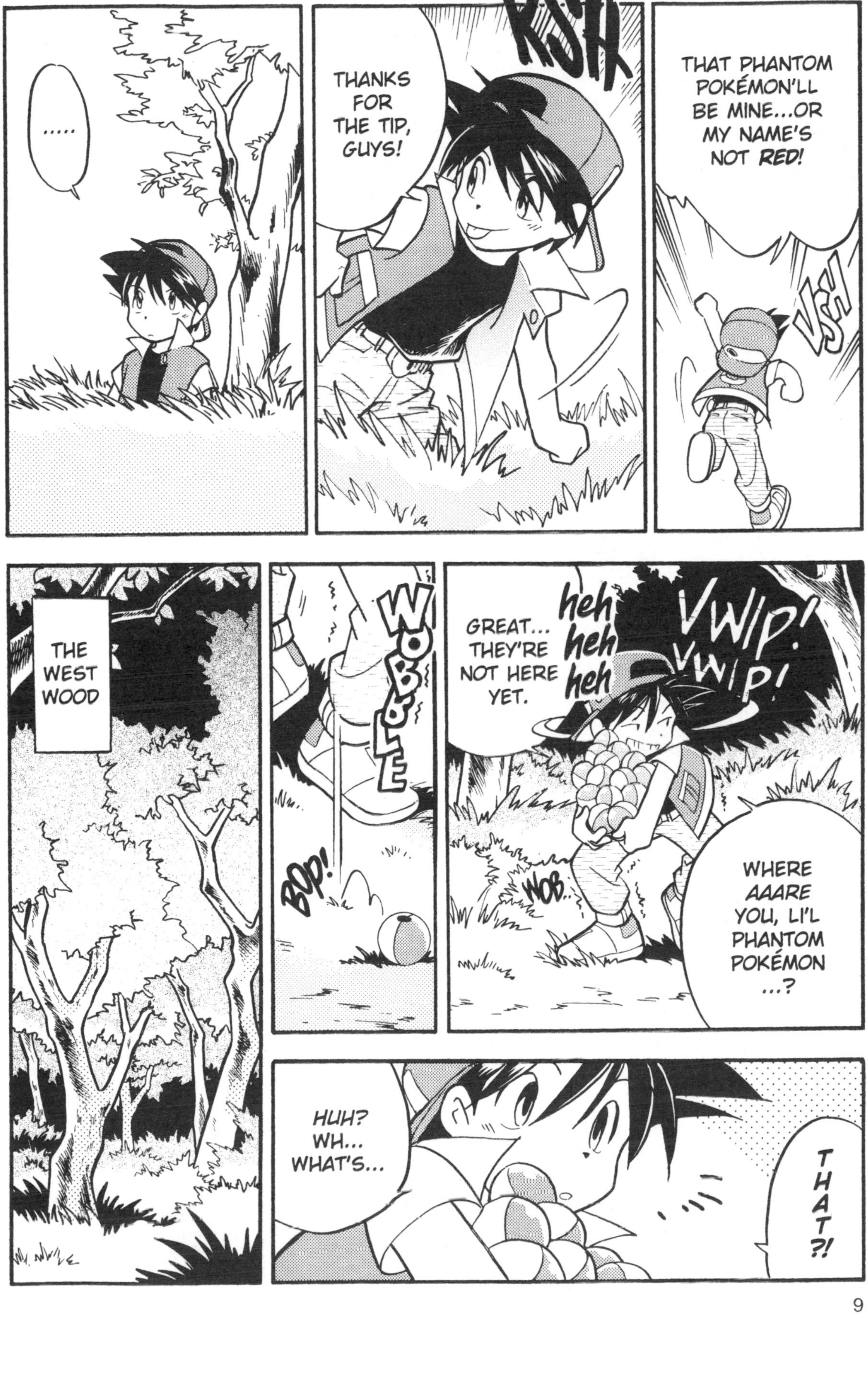
.....
THANKS FOR THE TIP, GUYS!
KSH
THAT PHANTOM POKÉMON'LL BE MINE...OR MY NAME'S NOT RED!
VSH
THE WEST WOOD
WOBBLE
BOP!
GREAT... THEY'RE NOT HERE YET.
heh heh heh
VWIP! VWIP!
WOB...
WHERE AAARE YOU, LI'L PHANTOM POKÉMON ...?
HUH? WH... WHAT'S...
THAT?!

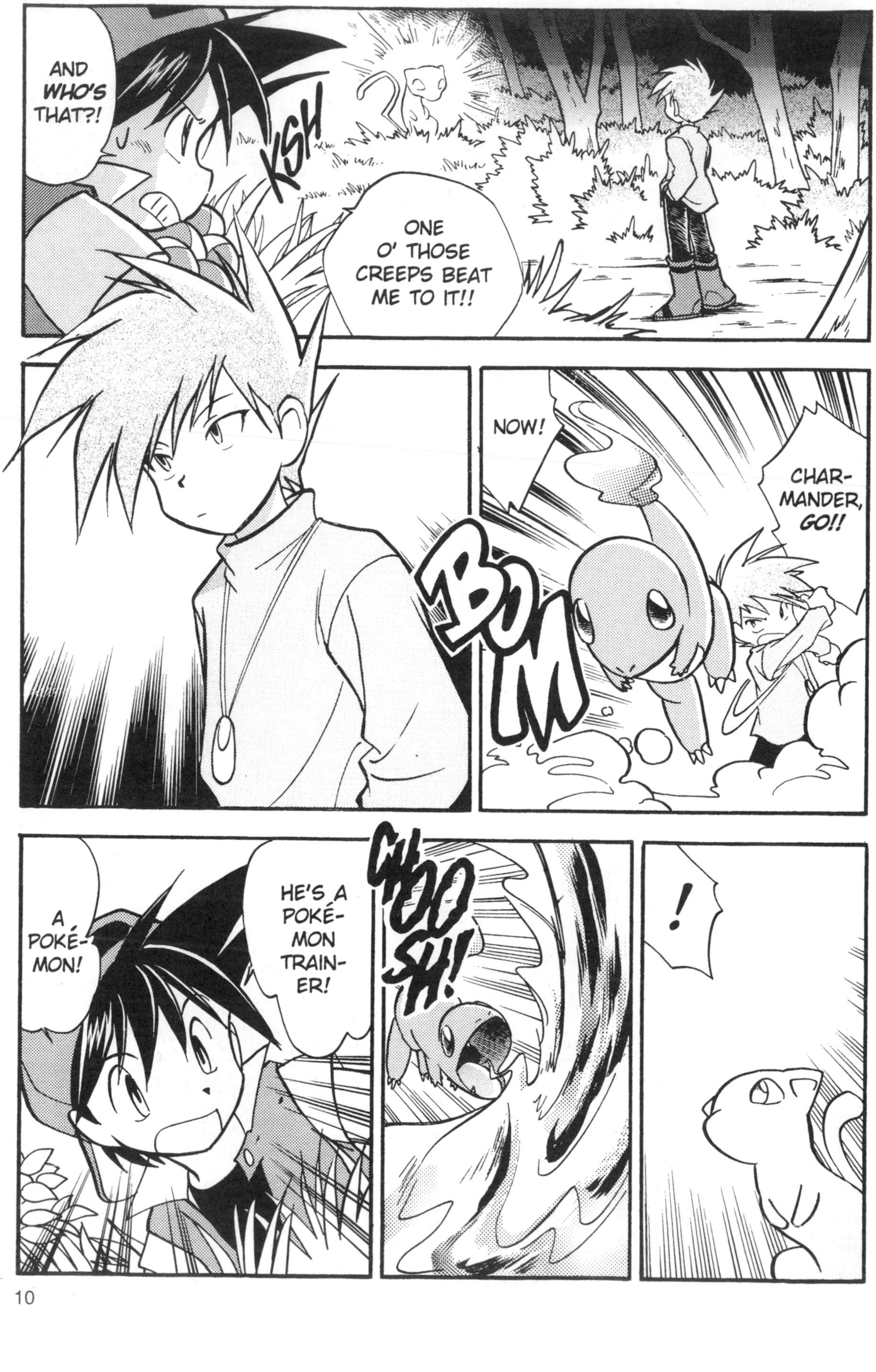
AND WHO'S THAT?!
KSH
ONE O' THOSE CREEPS BEAT ME TO IT!!
NOW!
CHAR-MANDER, GO!!
BOOM
A POKÉ-MON!
HE'S A POKÉ-MON TRAIN-ER!
CHOOSH!
!

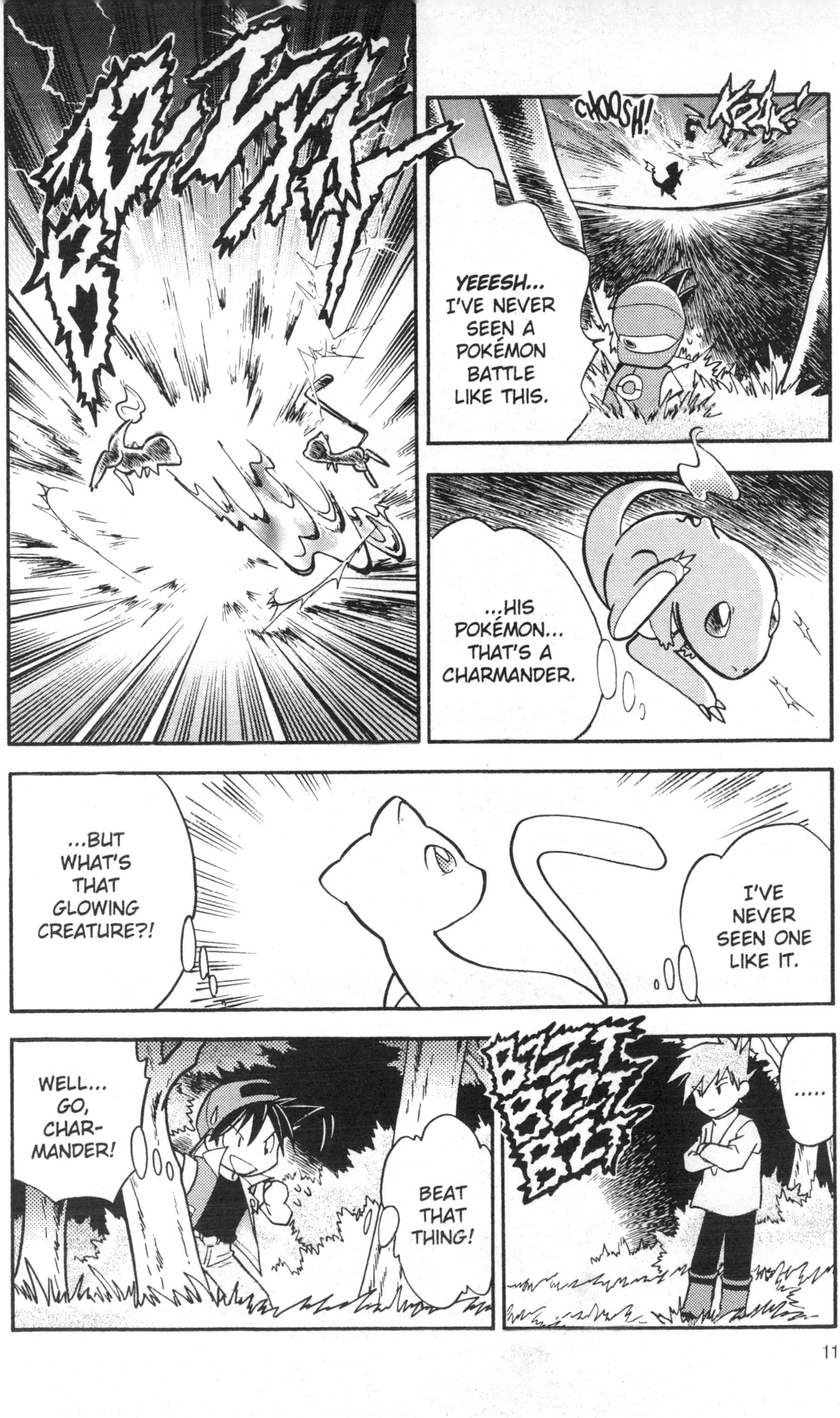
CHOOSH!
KRAK!
YEEESH... I'VE NEVER SEEN A POKÉMON BATTLE LIKE THIS.
...HIS POKÉMON... THAT'S A CHARMANDER.
...BUT WHAT'S THAT GLOWING CREATURE?!
I'VE NEVER SEEN ONE LIKE IT.
WELL... GO, CHAR-MANDER!
BEAT THAT THING!
.....

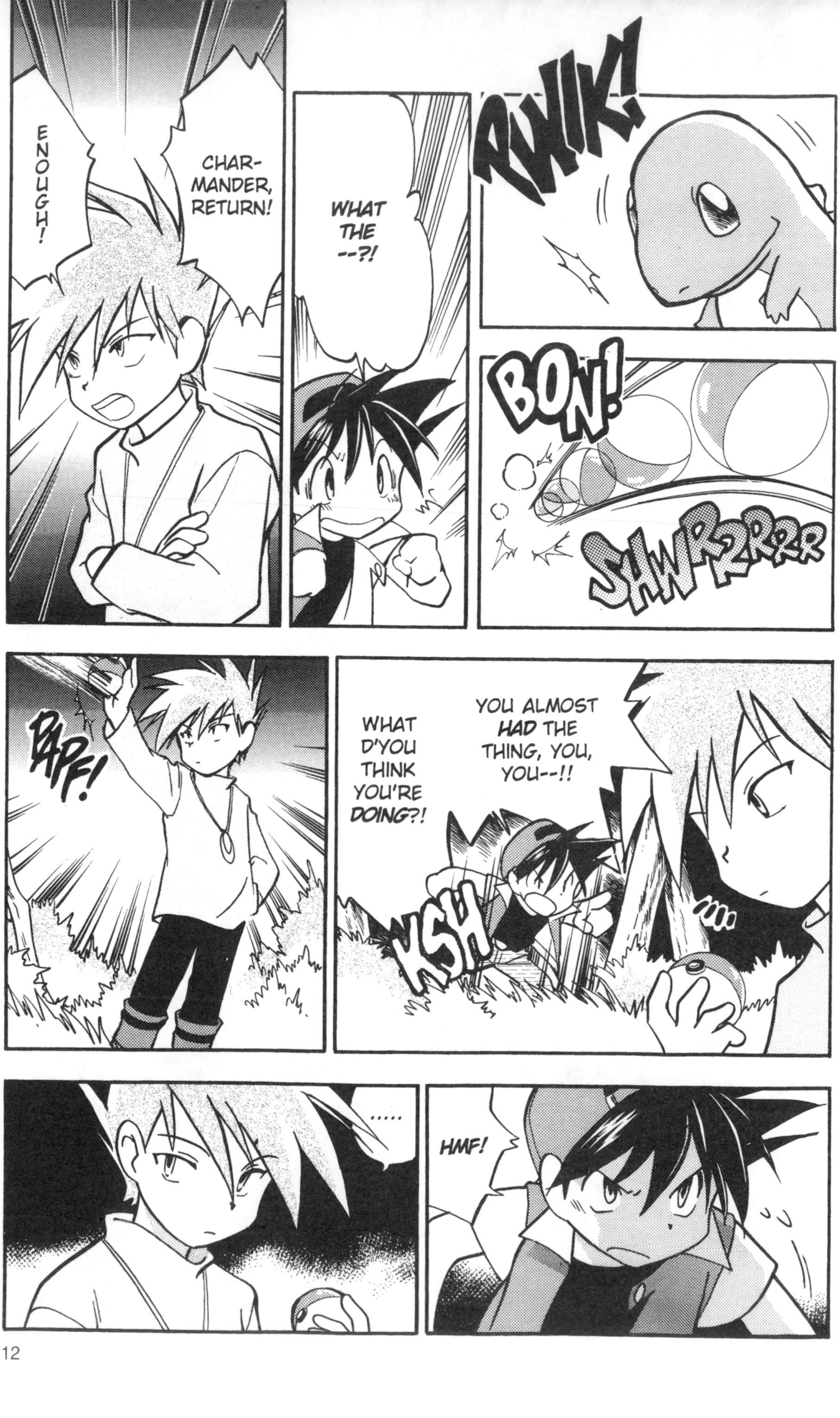
ENOUGH!
CHAR-MANDER, RETURN!
WHAT THE --?!
PWIK!
BON!
SHWRRRRR
PAPF!
WHAT D'YOU THINK YOU'RE DOING?!
YOU ALMOST HAD THE THING, YOU, YOU--!!
KSH
.....
HMF!

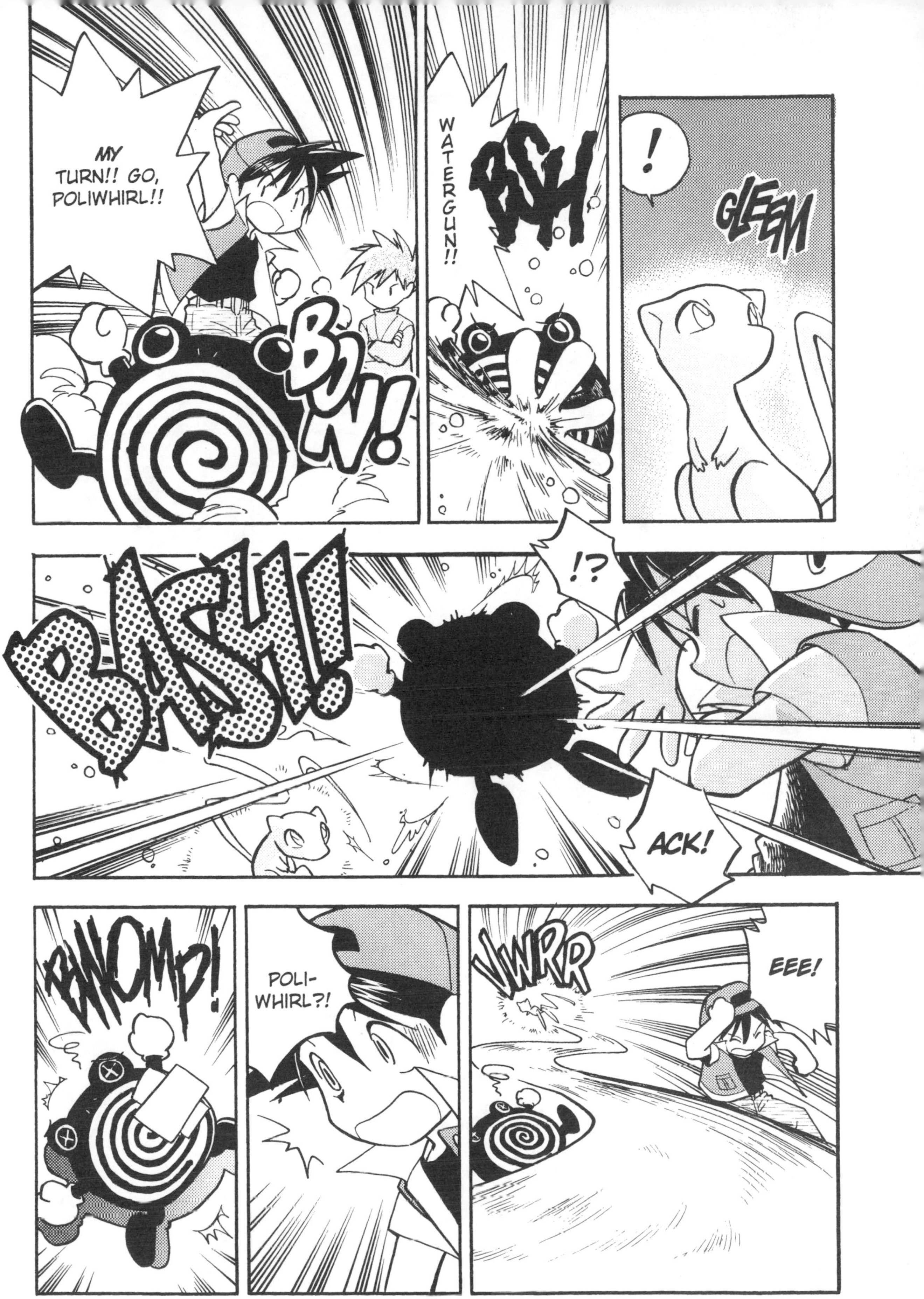
MY TURN!! GO, POLIWHIRL!!
BOON!
WATERGUN!!
BSH
!
GLEEM
BASH!
!?
ACK!
BWOMP!
POLI-WHIRL?!
VWRR
EEE!

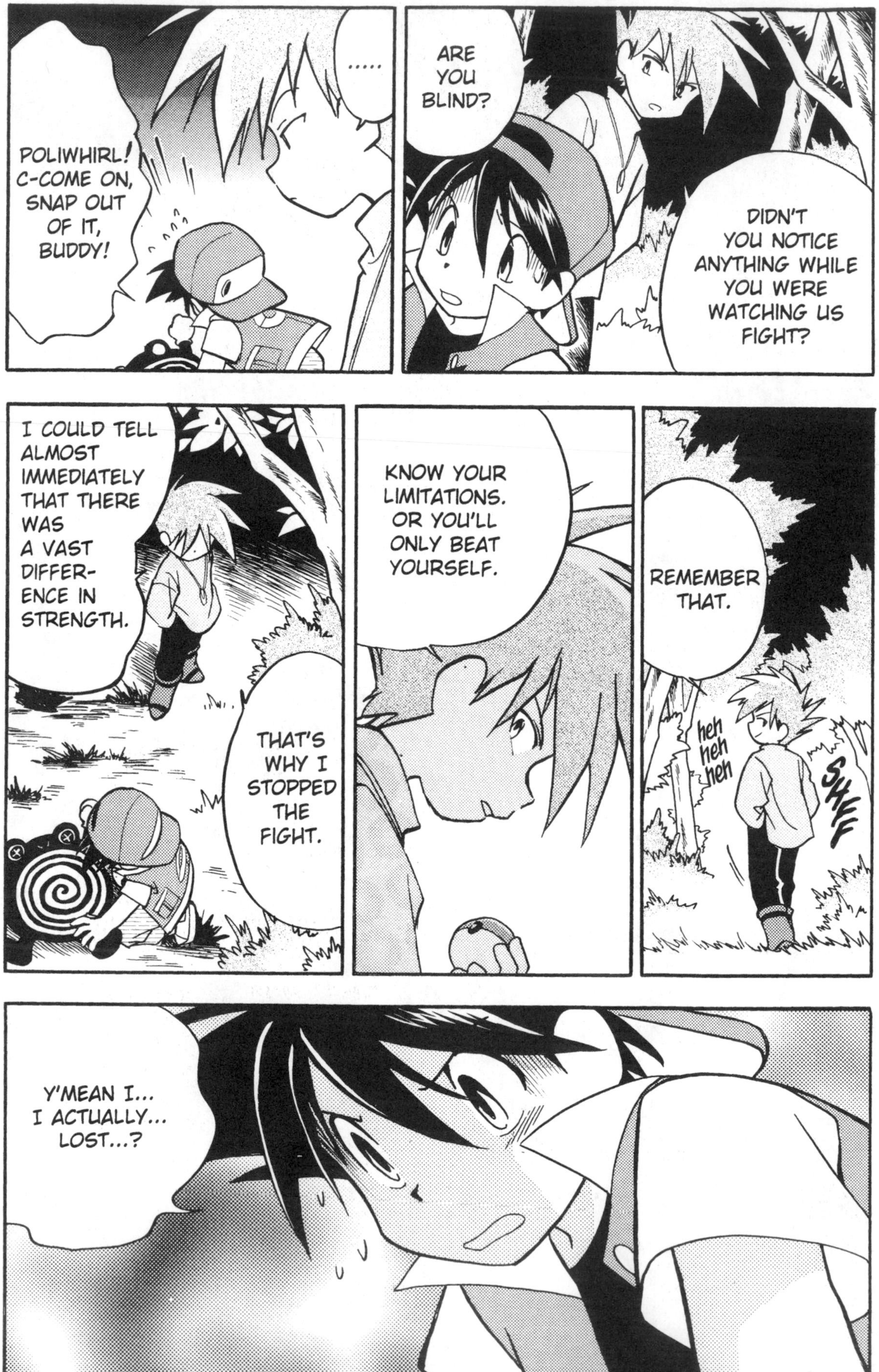
POLIWHIRL! C-COME ON, SNAP OUT OF IT, BUDDY!
.....
ARE YOU BLIND?
DIDN'T YOU NOTICE ANYTHING WHILE YOU WERE WATCHING US FIGHT?
I COULD TELL ALMOST IMMEDIATELY THAT THERE WAS A VAST DIFFER-ENCE IN STRENGTH.
THAT'S WHY I STOPPED THE FIGHT.
KNOW YOUR LIMITATIONS. OR YOU'LL ONLY BEAT YOURSELF.
REMEMBER THAT.
heh heh heh
Y'MEAN I... I ACTUALLY... LOST...?

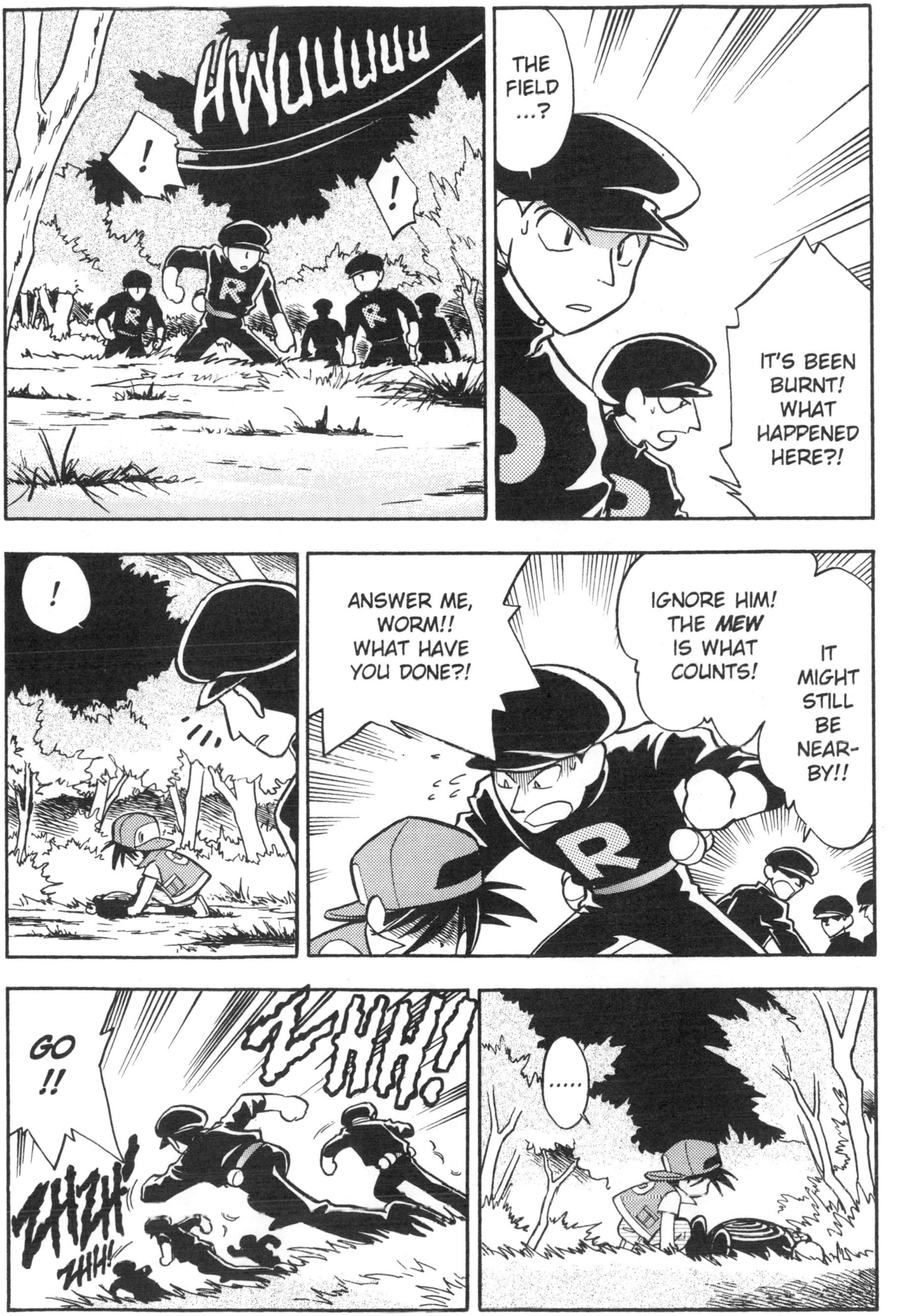
AWUUUUUU
!
!
THE FIELD ...?
IT'S BEEN BURNT! WHAT HAPPENED HERE?!
!
ANSWER ME, WORM!! WHAT HAVE YOU DONE?!
IGNORE HIM! THE MEW IS WHAT COUNTS!
IT MIGHT STILL BE NEAR-BY!!
GO !!
ZHHH!
ZHZH ZHH!
......

SHHP

SO THIS IS OL' PROF OAK'S LAB...

OAK POKÉMON RESEARCH LAB

THEY SAY HE'S A MEAN OLD GUY...

...SO I ALWAYS KEPT AWAY...

BUT I GUESS THE ONLY PLACE I'LL LEARN TO BE A GREAT POKEMON TRAINER...

IS HERE.

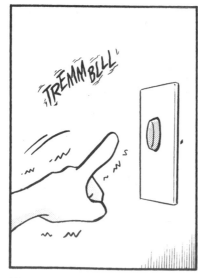

TREMMBLL

Biing Bonng!

gvmmp

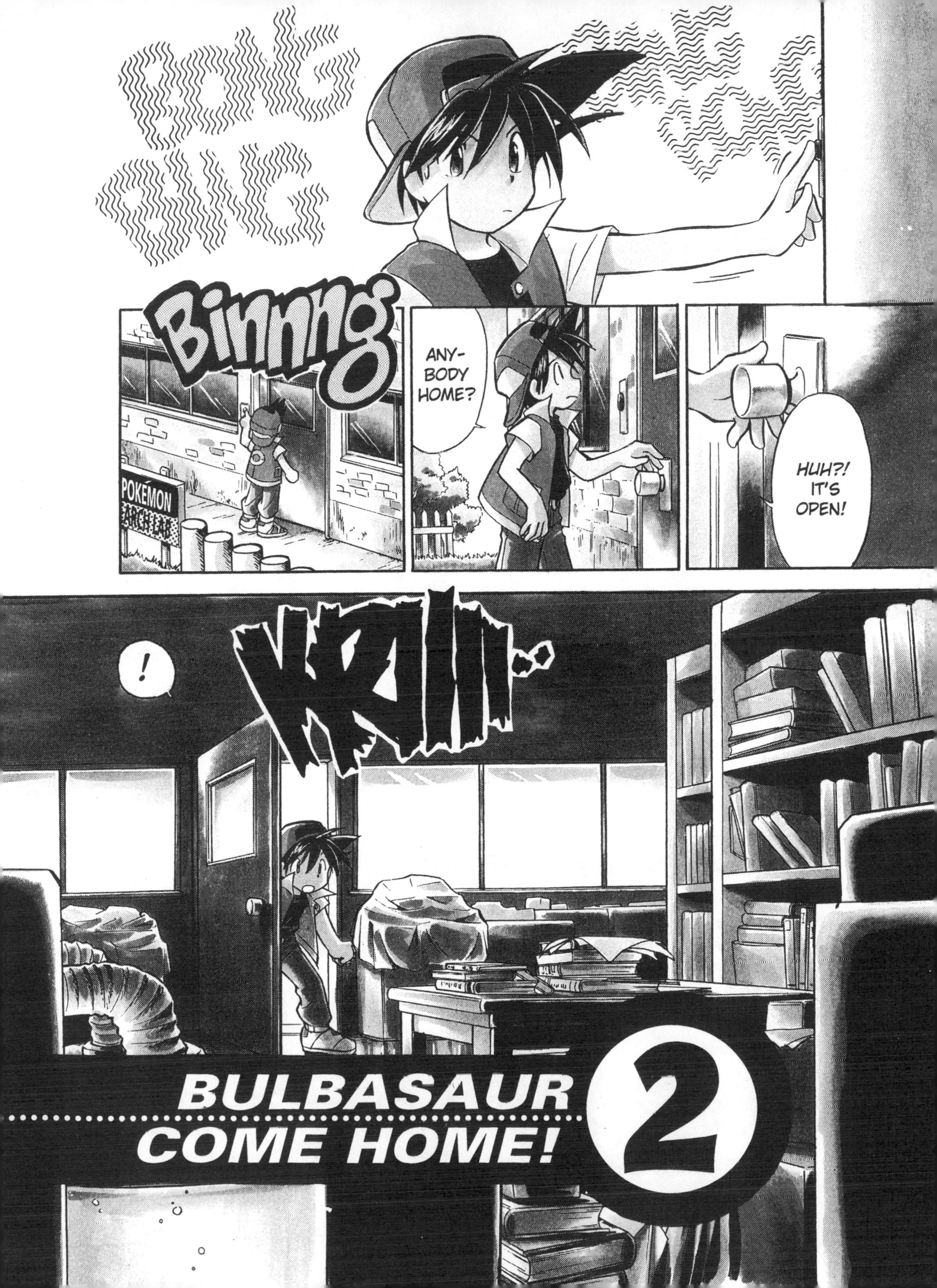
Binnng
POKÉMON
ANY-BODY HOME?
HUH?! IT'S OPEN!
!
BULBASAUR COME HOME!
2

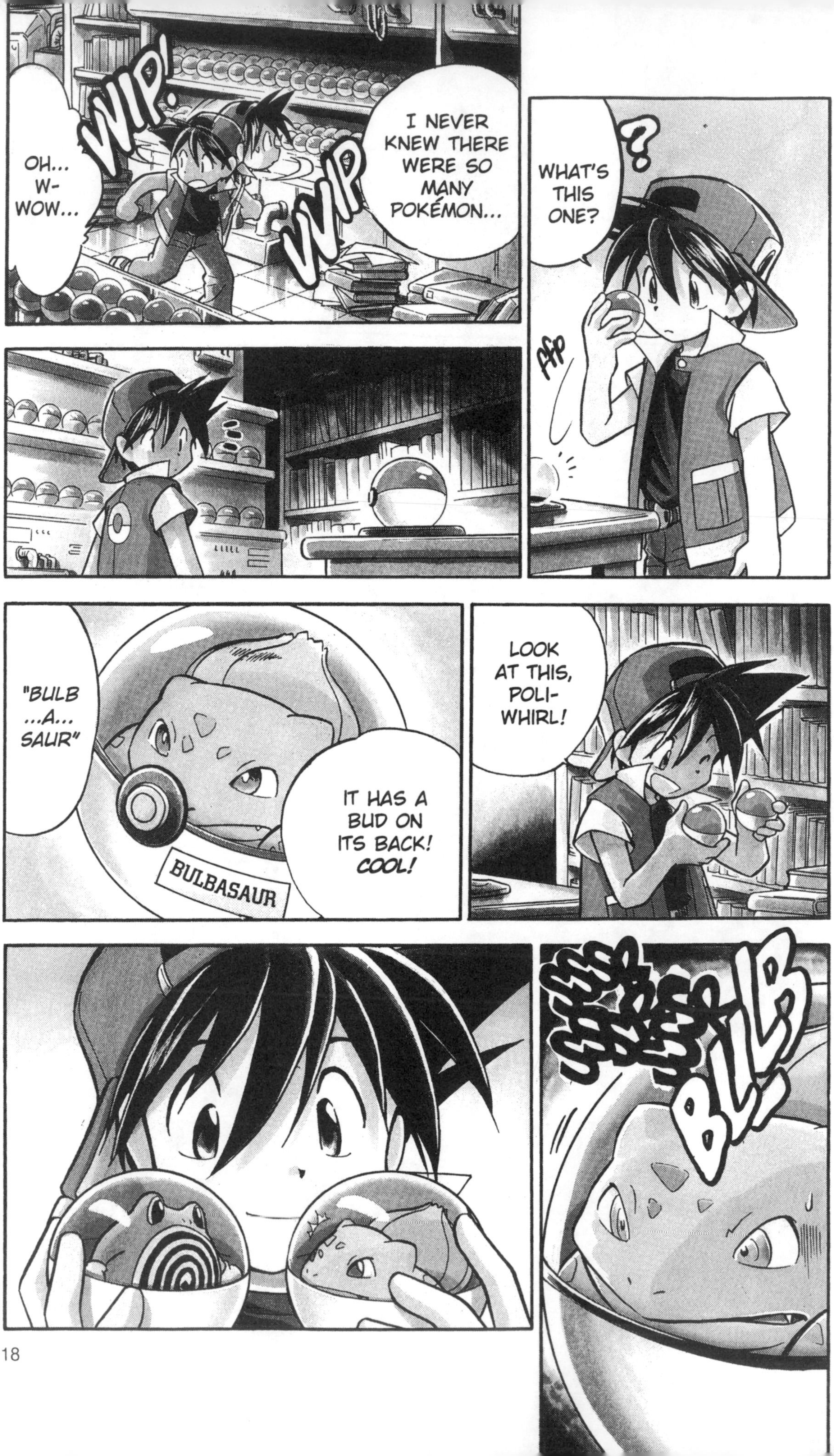
VVIP!
OH... W-WOW...
I NEVER KNEW THERE WERE SO MANY POKÉMON...
VVIP
?
WHAT'S THIS ONE?
FFP
"BULB ...A... SAUR"
BULBASAUR
IT HAS A BUD ON ITS BACK! COOL!
LOOK AT THIS, POLI-WHIRL!
BULB

KRII

eh?

YOU... YOU... POKÉ-THIEF!

W...WAIT, N-NO...I ...I...I MEAN I...

DOMP! DOMP!

TR'P!

WAAA...

NO, YOU IDIOT!!

WH-WH-WH-?!

PSHHHHHHH

B-B-BOING!

EE-YAAAAA!!

19

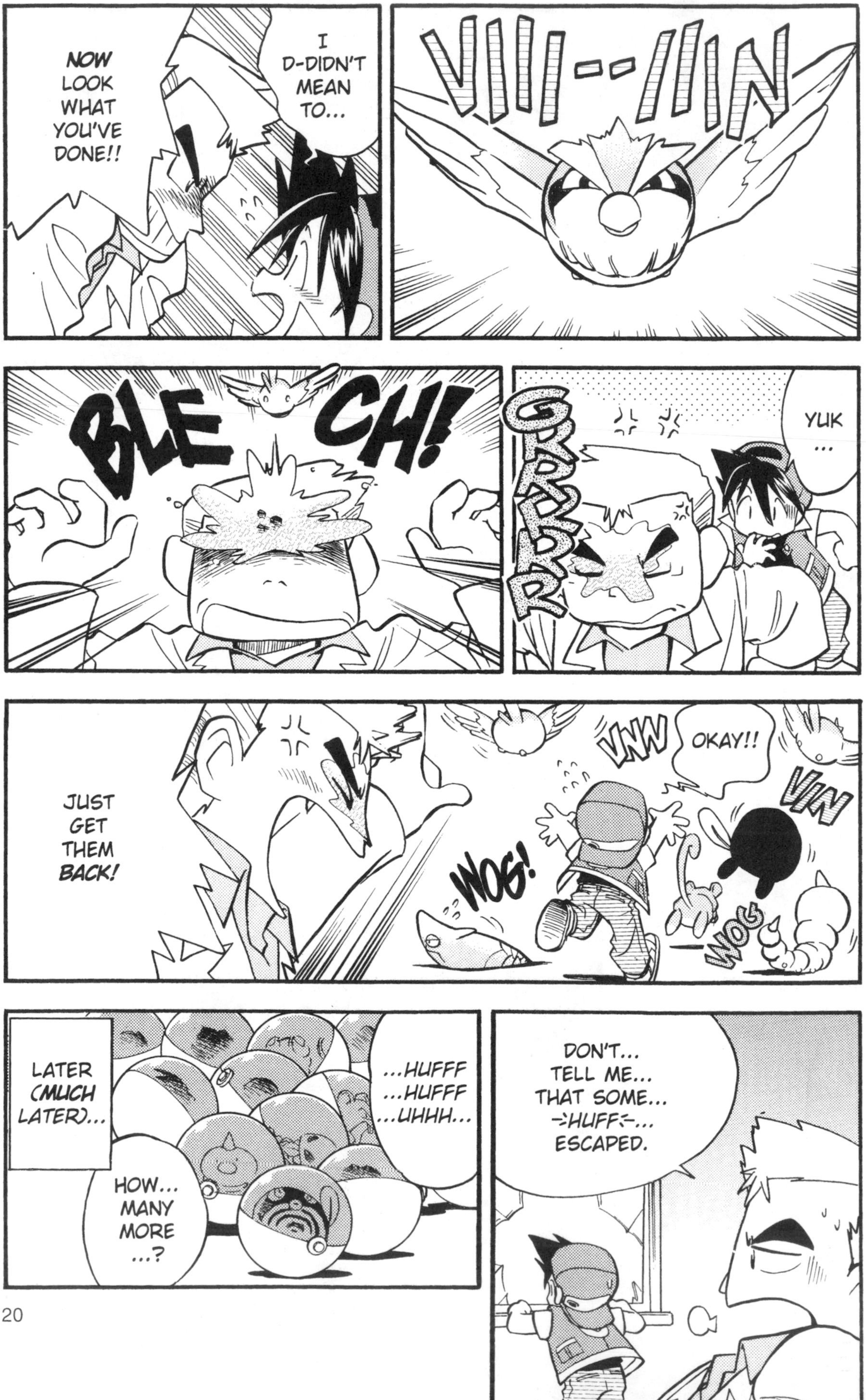

NOW LOOK WHAT YOU'VE DONE!!
I D-DIDN'T MEAN TO...
VIII--IIIN
BLE CH!
GRRRRR
YUK ...
JUST GET THEM BACK!
VNN
OKAY!!
VIN
WOG!
WOG
LATER (MUCH LATER)...
...HUFFF ...HUFFF ...UHHH...
HOW... MANY MORE ...?
DON'T... TELL ME... THAT SOME... -HUFF-... ESCAPED.

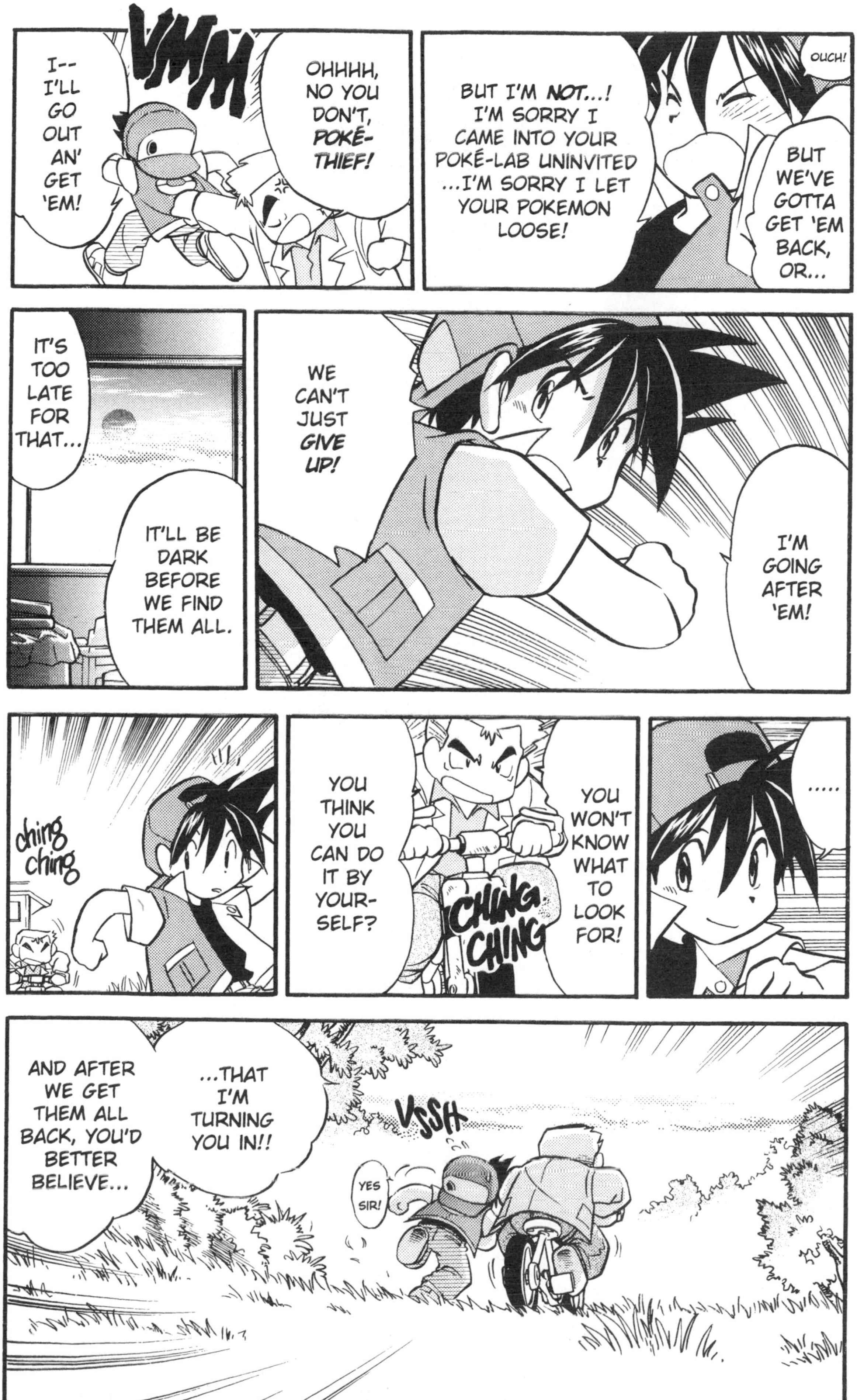

I-- I'LL GO OUT AN' GET 'EM!
VMM
OHHHH, NO YOU DON'T, POKÉ-THIEF!
BUT I'M NOT...! I'M SORRY I CAME INTO YOUR POKÉ-LAB UNINVITED ...I'M SORRY I LET YOUR POKEMON LOOSE!
OUCH!
BUT WE'VE GOTTA GET 'EM BACK, OR...
IT'S TOO LATE FOR THAT...
IT'LL BE DARK BEFORE WE FIND THEM ALL.
WE CAN'T JUST GIVE UP!
I'M GOING AFTER 'EM!
ching ching
YOU THINK YOU CAN DO IT BY YOUR-SELF?
CHING CHING
YOU WON'T KNOW WHAT TO LOOK FOR!
.....
AND AFTER WE GET THEM ALL BACK, YOU'D BETTER BELIEVE...
...THAT I'M TURNING YOU IN!!
VSSH
YES SIR!

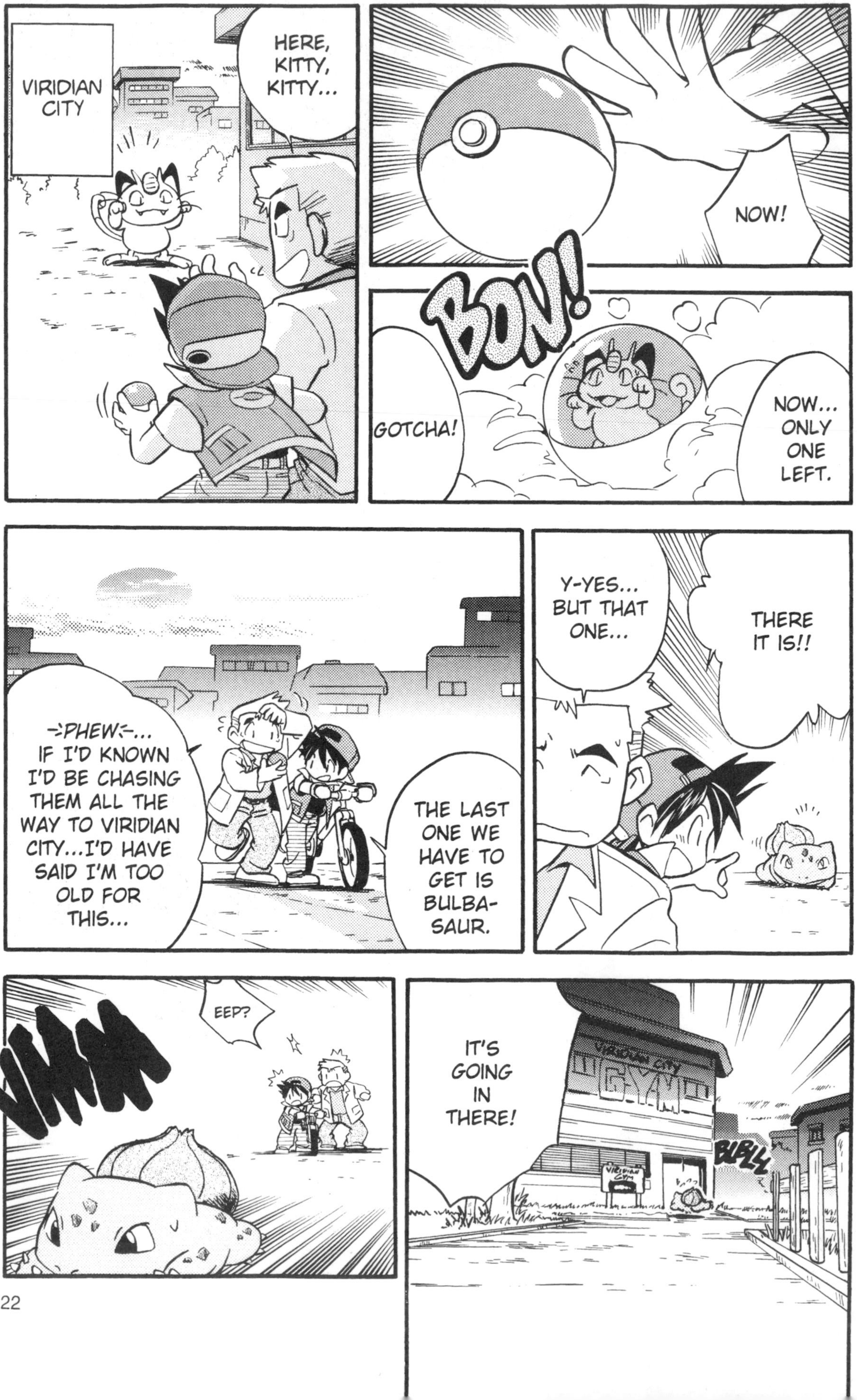
VIRIDIAN CITY
HERE, KITTY, KITTY...
NOW!
BON!
GOTCHA!
NOW... ONLY ONE LEFT.
Y-YES... BUT THAT ONE...
THERE IT IS!!
-PHEW-... IF I'D KNOWN I'D BE CHASING THEM ALL THE WAY TO VIRIDIAN CITY...I'D HAVE SAID I'M TOO OLD FOR THIS...
THE LAST ONE WE HAVE TO GET IS BULBA-SAUR.
EEP?
IT'S GOING IN THERE!
VIRIDIAN CITY GYM
BUBLL

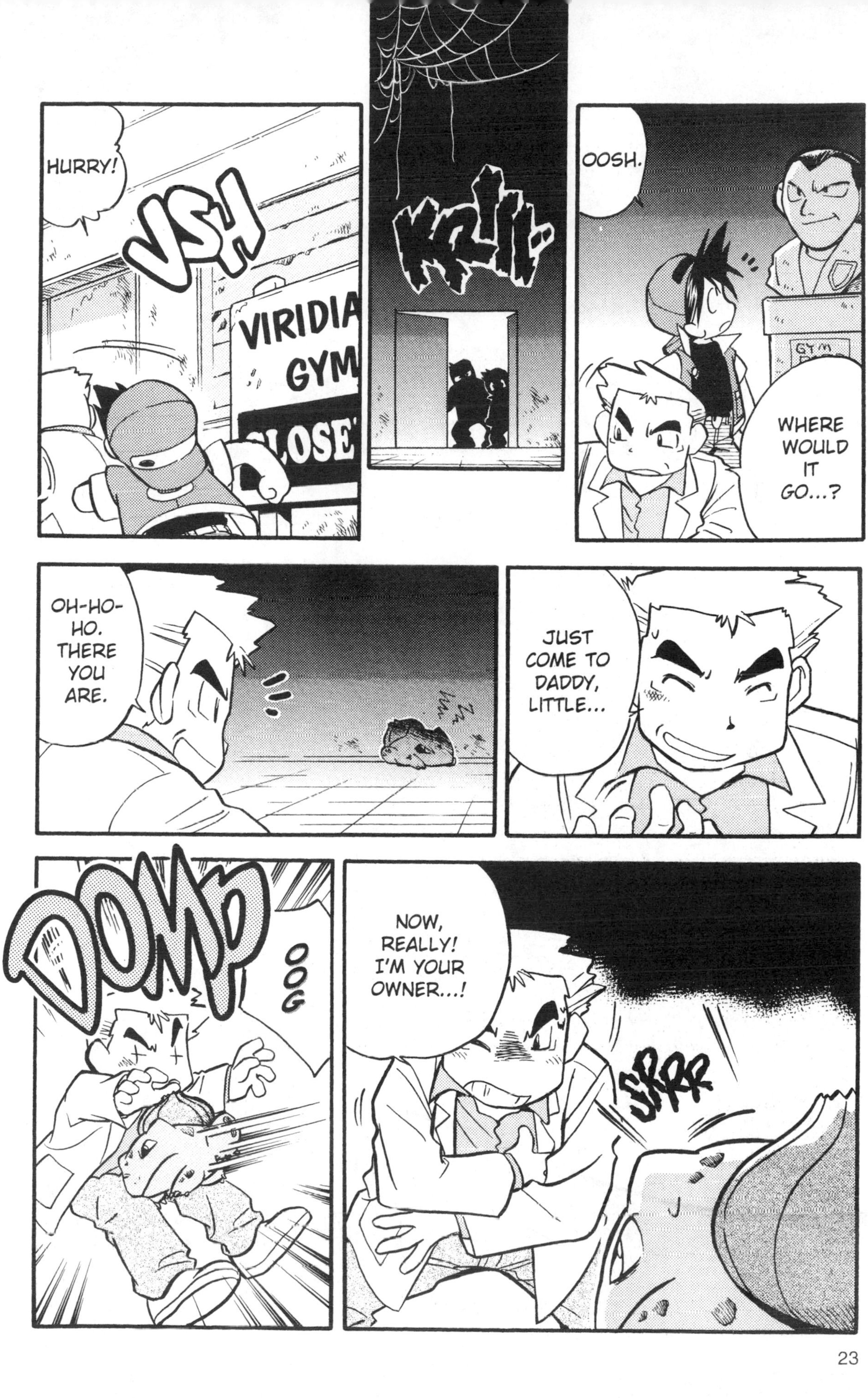
HURRY!
VSH
VIRIDIAN GYM
CLOSED
KRIII
OOSH.
GYM
WHERE WOULD IT GO...?
OH-HO-HO. THERE YOU ARE.
JUST COME TO DADDY, LITTLE...
DOMP
OOG
NOW, REALLY! I'M YOUR OWNER...!
SRRR

BLB? VIP

DON'T BE AFRAID, BULBASAUR.

...... OF COURSE YOU'RE NERVOUS...

IT'S THE FIRST TIME YOU'VE BEEN OUTSIDE.

YOU WERE KEPT SEPARATE FROM THE OTHERS IN THE POKÉ-LAB, WEREN'T YOU?

I'LL BET YOU'D NEVER SEEN ANOTHER LIVING THING BESIDES THE OL' PROF, HUH?

......

YEAH, THAT'S A GOOD BOY. ARE YOU HUNGRY?

......

prrrr prrrr

KRI

!?

!!

GASP!

I-IT'S...

A WILD MACHOKE!!

MMMMAAAA

YAA!!

WOOO

SSSRRRRD

BU

CHKK

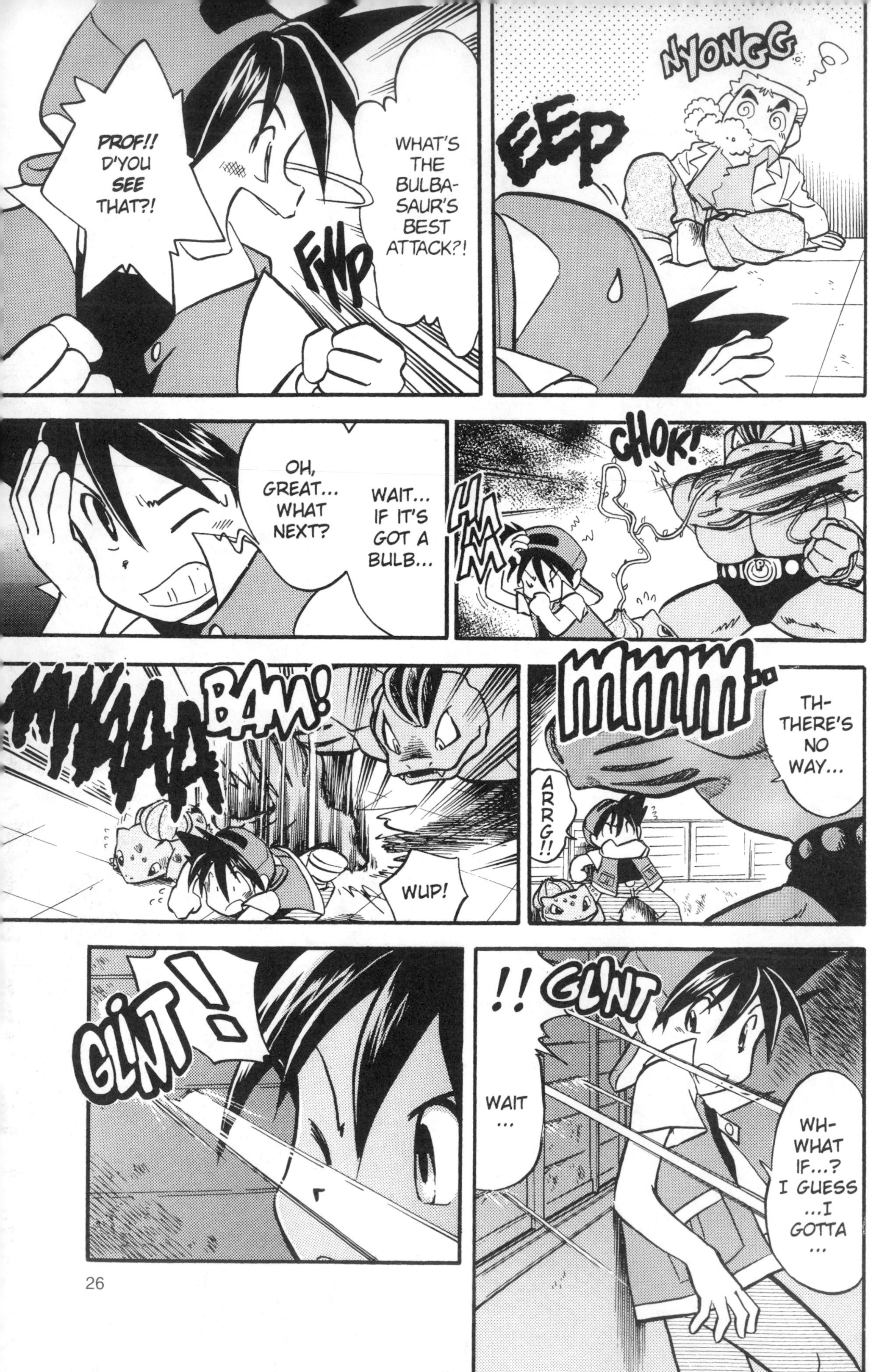
PROF!! D'YOU SEE THAT?!
WHAT'S THE BULBASAUR'S BEST ATTACK?!
FWP
NYONGG
EEP
OH, GREAT... WHAT NEXT?
WAIT... IF IT'S GOT A BULB...
CHOK!
HMMM
WHAAA
BAM!
WUP!
MMMM..
TH-THERE'S NO WAY...
ARRG!!
GLINT!
!! GLINT
WAIT ...
WH-WHAT IF...? I GUESS ...I GOTTA ...

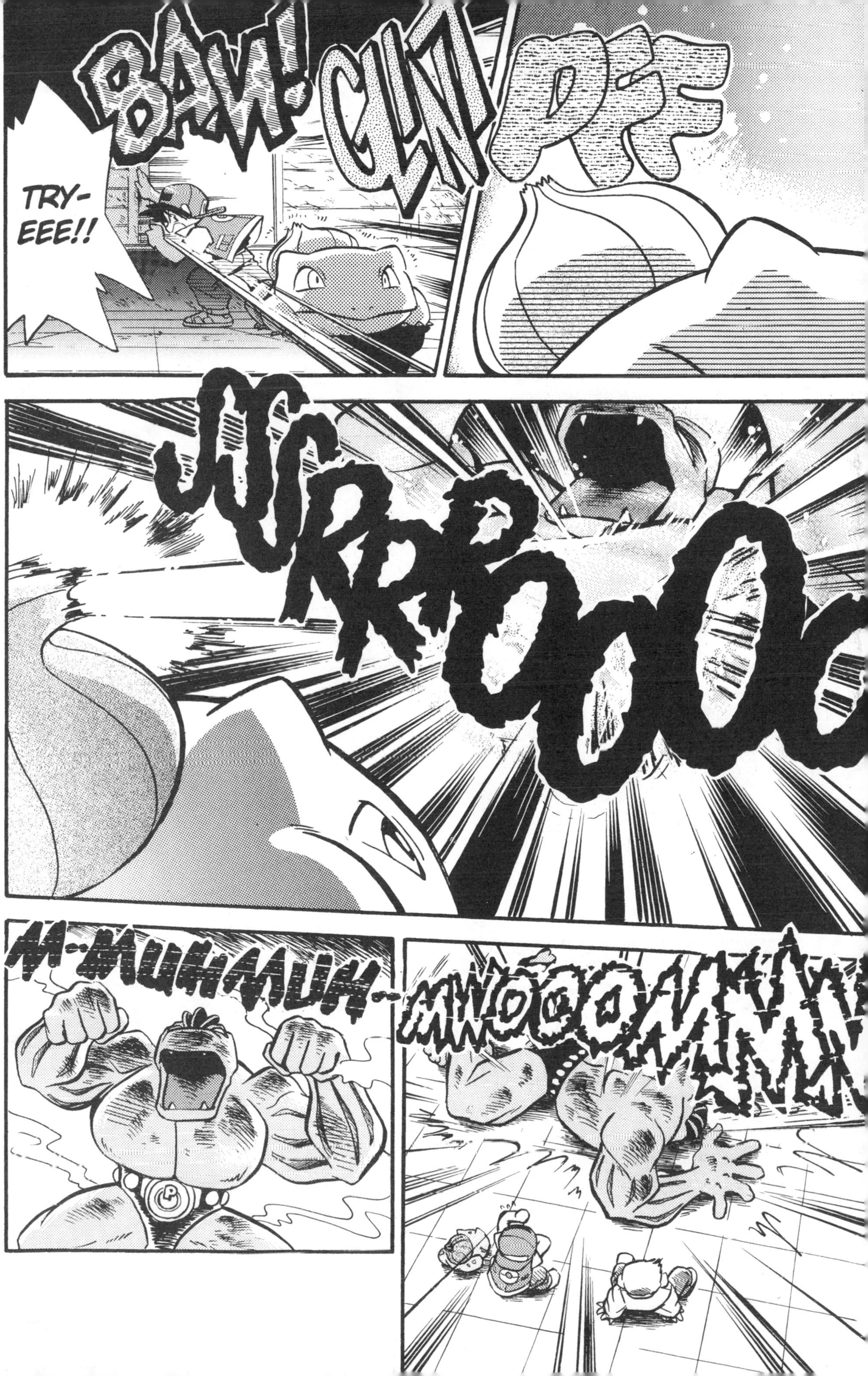
TRY-
EEE!!
BAM!
M-MUHMUH-

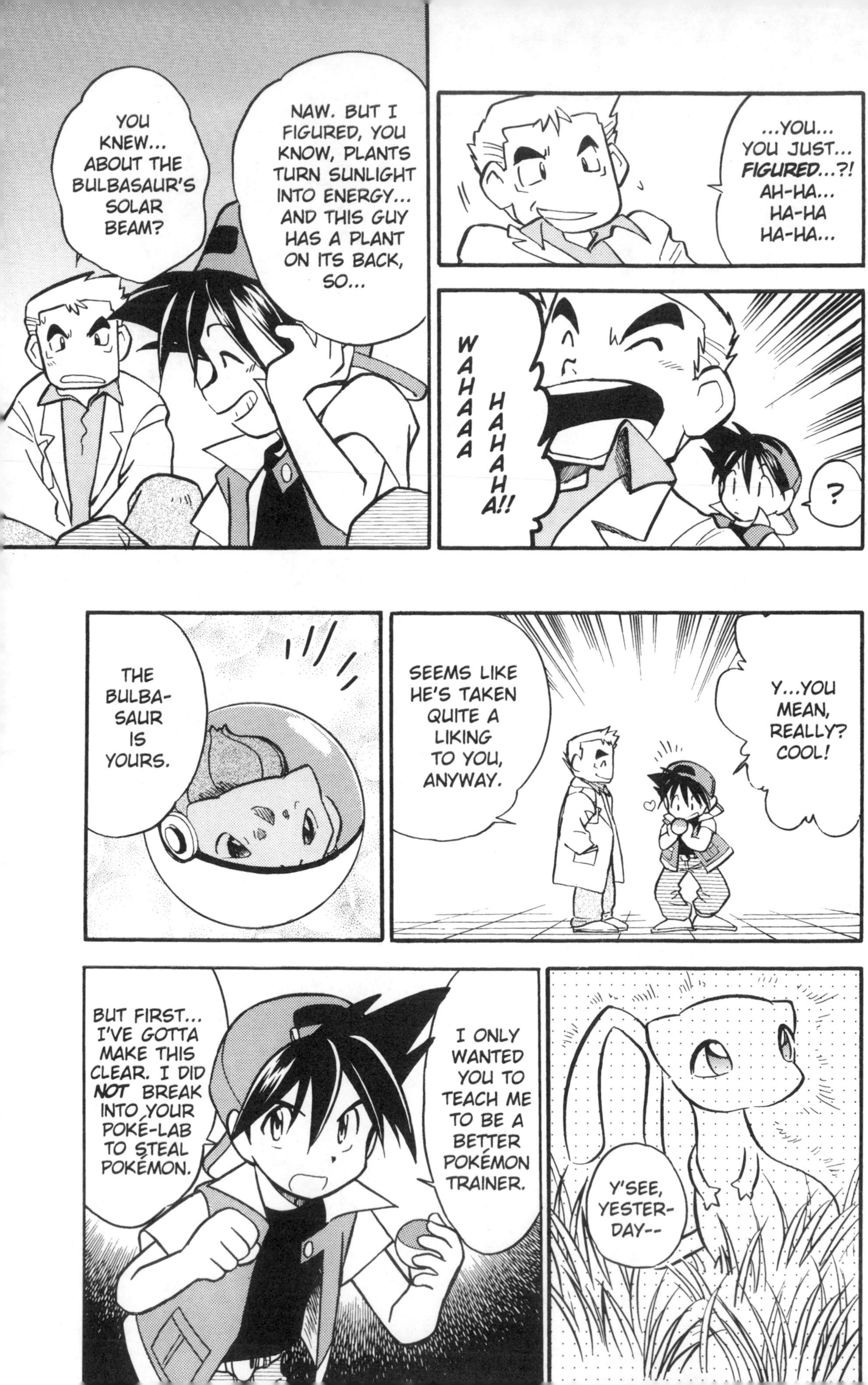
YOU KNEW... ABOUT THE BULBASAUR'S SOLAR BEAM?
NAW. BUT I FIGURED, YOU KNOW, PLANTS TURN SUNLIGHT INTO ENERGY... AND THIS GUY HAS A PLANT ON ITS BACK, SO...
...YOU... YOU JUST... FIGURED...?! AH-HA... HA-HA HA-HA...
WAHAAAA HAHAHAHA!!
?
THE BULBA-SAUR IS YOURS.
SEEMS LIKE HE'S TAKEN QUITE A LIKING TO YOU, ANYWAY.
Y...YOU MEAN, REALLY? COOL!
BUT FIRST... I'VE GOTTA MAKE THIS CLEAR. I DID NOT BREAK INTO YOUR POKÉ-LAB TO STEAL POKÉMON.
I ONLY WANTED YOU TO TEACH ME TO BE A BETTER POKÉMON TRAINER.
Y'SEE, YESTER-DAY--

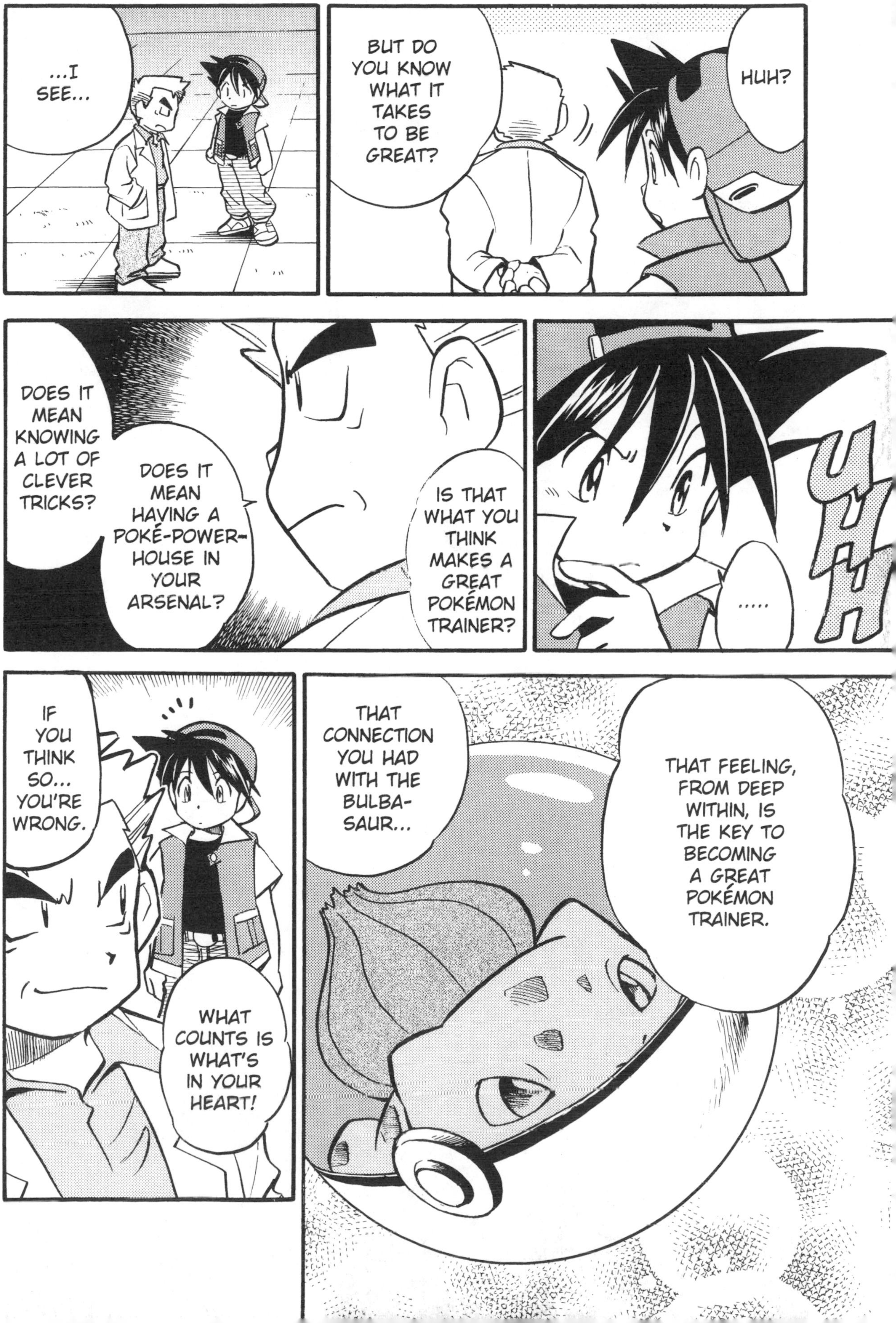
...I SEE...
BUT DO YOU KNOW WHAT IT TAKES TO BE GREAT?
HUH?
DOES IT MEAN KNOWING A LOT OF CLEVER TRICKS?
DOES IT MEAN HAVING A POKÉ-POWER-HOUSE IN YOUR ARSENAL?
IS THAT WHAT YOU THINK MAKES A GREAT POKÉMON TRAINER?
UHH
.....
IF YOU THINK SO... YOU'RE WRONG.
WHAT COUNTS IS WHAT'S IN YOUR HEART!
THAT CONNECTION YOU HAD WITH THE BULBA-SAUR...
THAT FEELING, FROM DEEP WITHIN, IS THE KEY TO BECOMING A GREAT POKÉMON TRAINER.

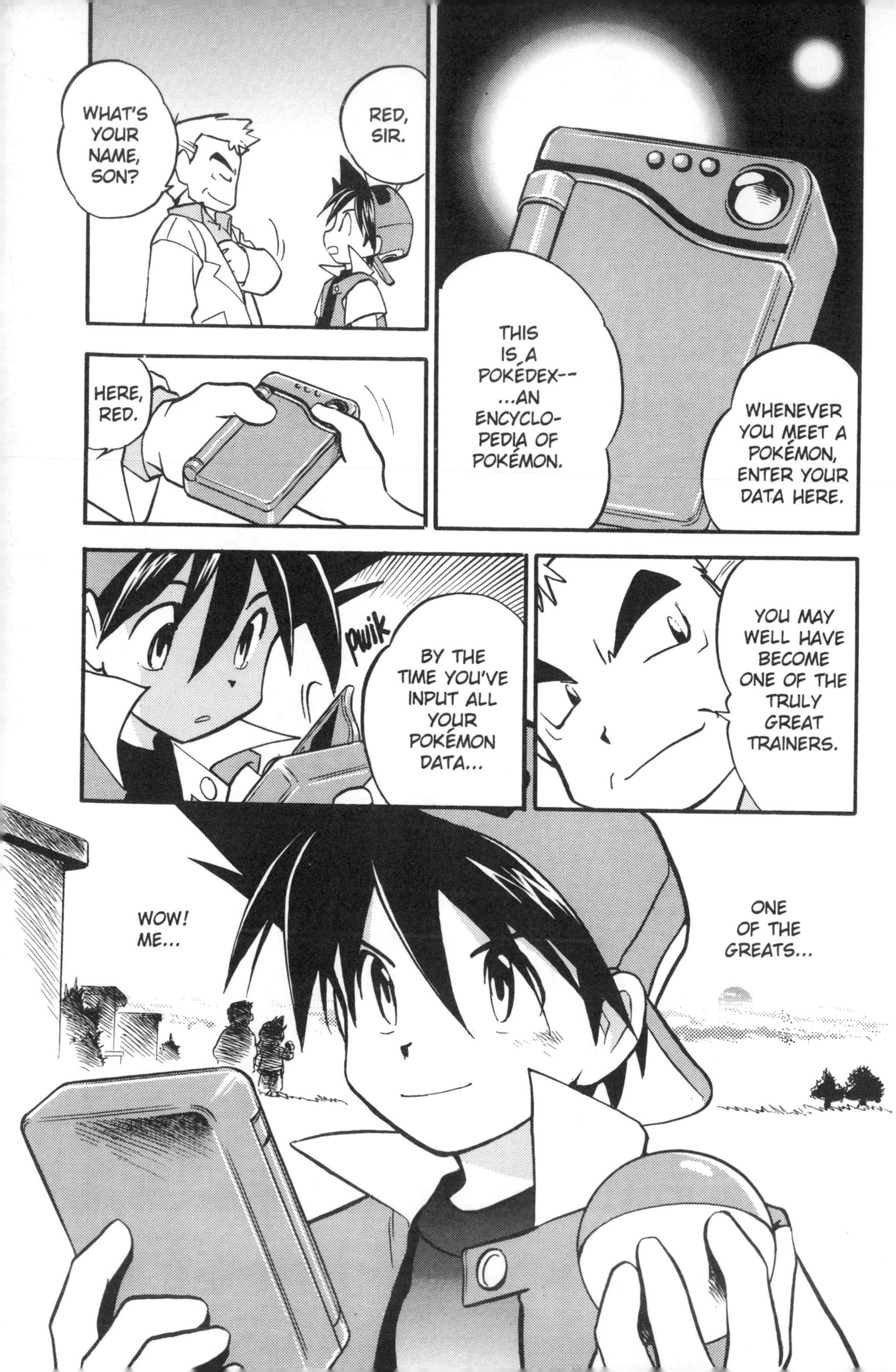
WHAT'S YOUR NAME, SON?
RED, SIR.
THIS IS A POKÉDEX-- ...AN ENCYCLOPEDIA OF POKÉMON.
WHENEVER YOU MEET A POKÉMON, ENTER YOUR DATA HERE.
HERE, RED.
pwik
BY THE TIME YOU'VE INPUT ALL YOUR POKÉMON DATA...
YOU MAY WELL HAVE BECOME ONE OF THE TRULY GREAT TRAINERS.
WOW! ME...
ONE OF THE GREATS...

CHAPTER 3

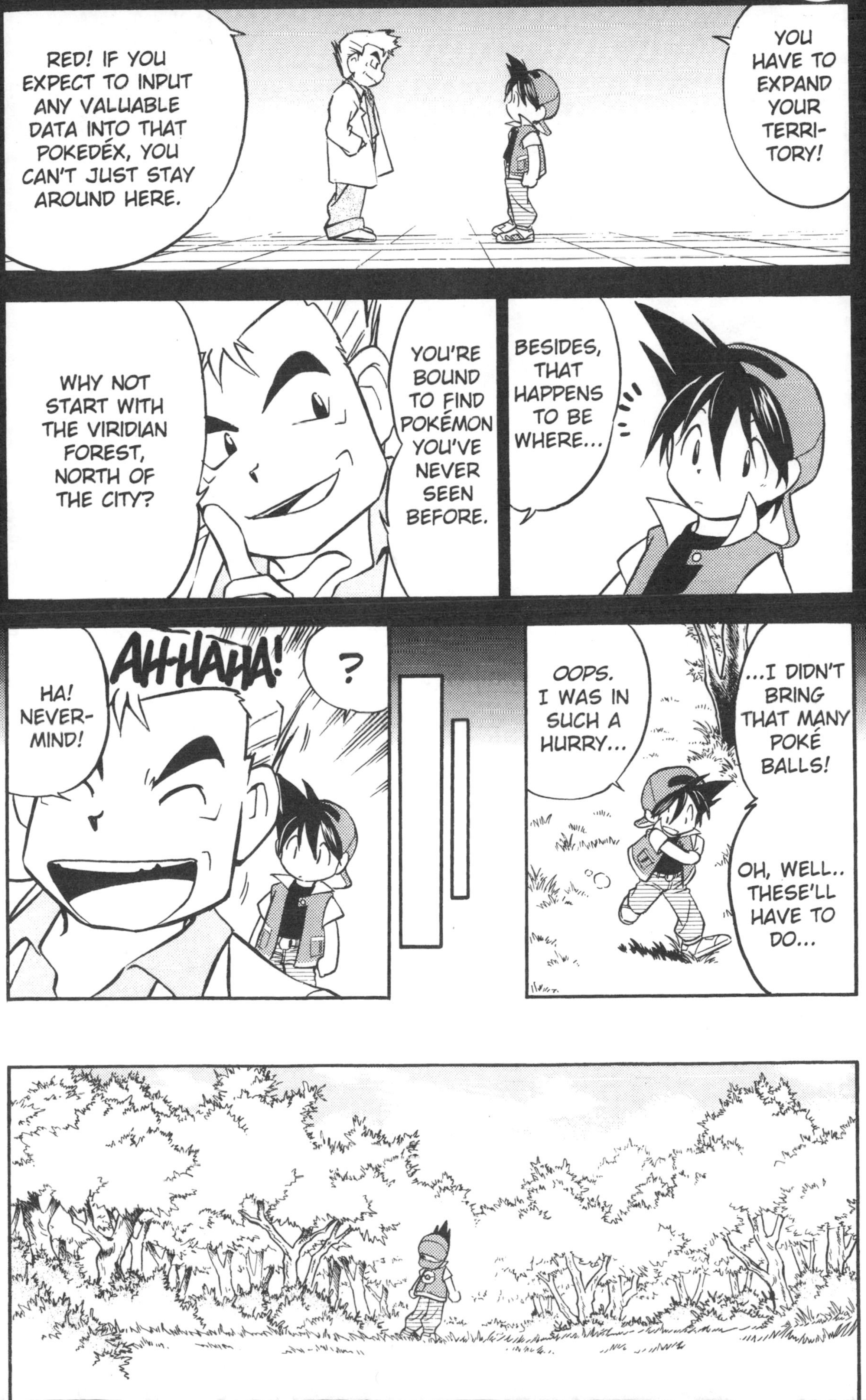
RED! IF YOU EXPECT TO INPUT ANY VALUABLE DATA INTO THAT POKEDÉX, YOU CAN'T JUST STAY AROUND HERE.
YOU HAVE TO EXPAND YOUR TERRI-TORY!
WHY NOT START WITH THE VIRIDIAN FOREST, NORTH OF THE CITY?
YOU'RE BOUND TO FIND POKÉMON YOU'VE NEVER SEEN BEFORE.
BESIDES, THAT HAPPENS TO BE WHERE...
HA! NEVER-MIND!
AH-HAHA!
?
OOPS. I WAS IN SUCH A HURRY...
...I DIDN'T BRING THAT MANY POKÉ BALLS!
OH, WELL.. THESE'LL HAVE TO DO...

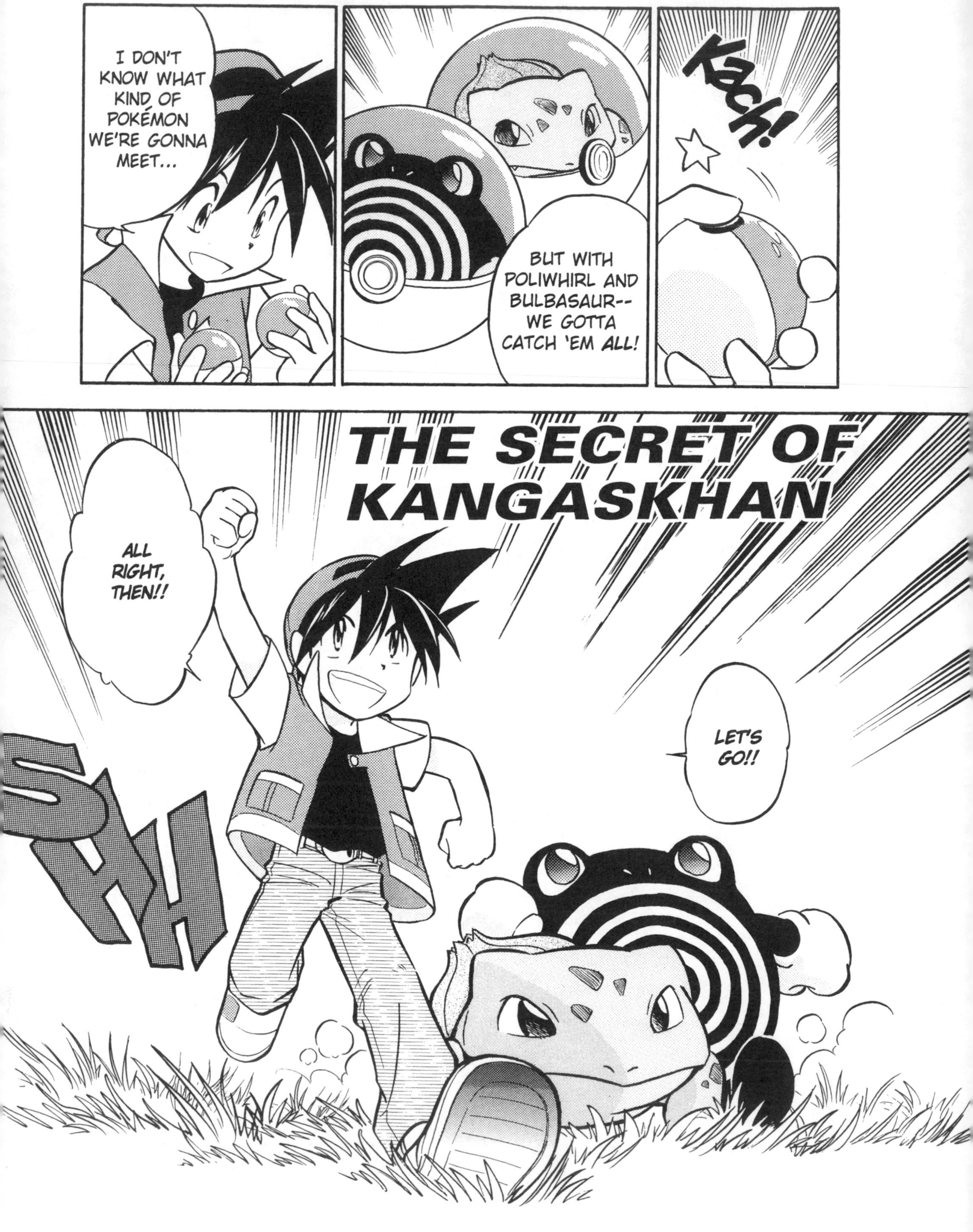

I DON'T KNOW WHAT KIND OF POKÉMON WE'RE GONNA MEET...
BUT WITH POLIWHIRL AND BULBASAUR-- WE GOTTA CATCH 'EM ALL!
KACH!
THE SECRET OF KANGASKHAN
ALL RIGHT, THEN!!
LET'S GO!!

THE
VIRIDIAN
FOREST

HSH

.....

KACH!

CHAR-
MANDER,
GO!!

CHOOSH

BON!

!

VWWN

.....

MONP!

SO...A
VENO-
MOTH...

FZZ

FZZ

FZZ

33

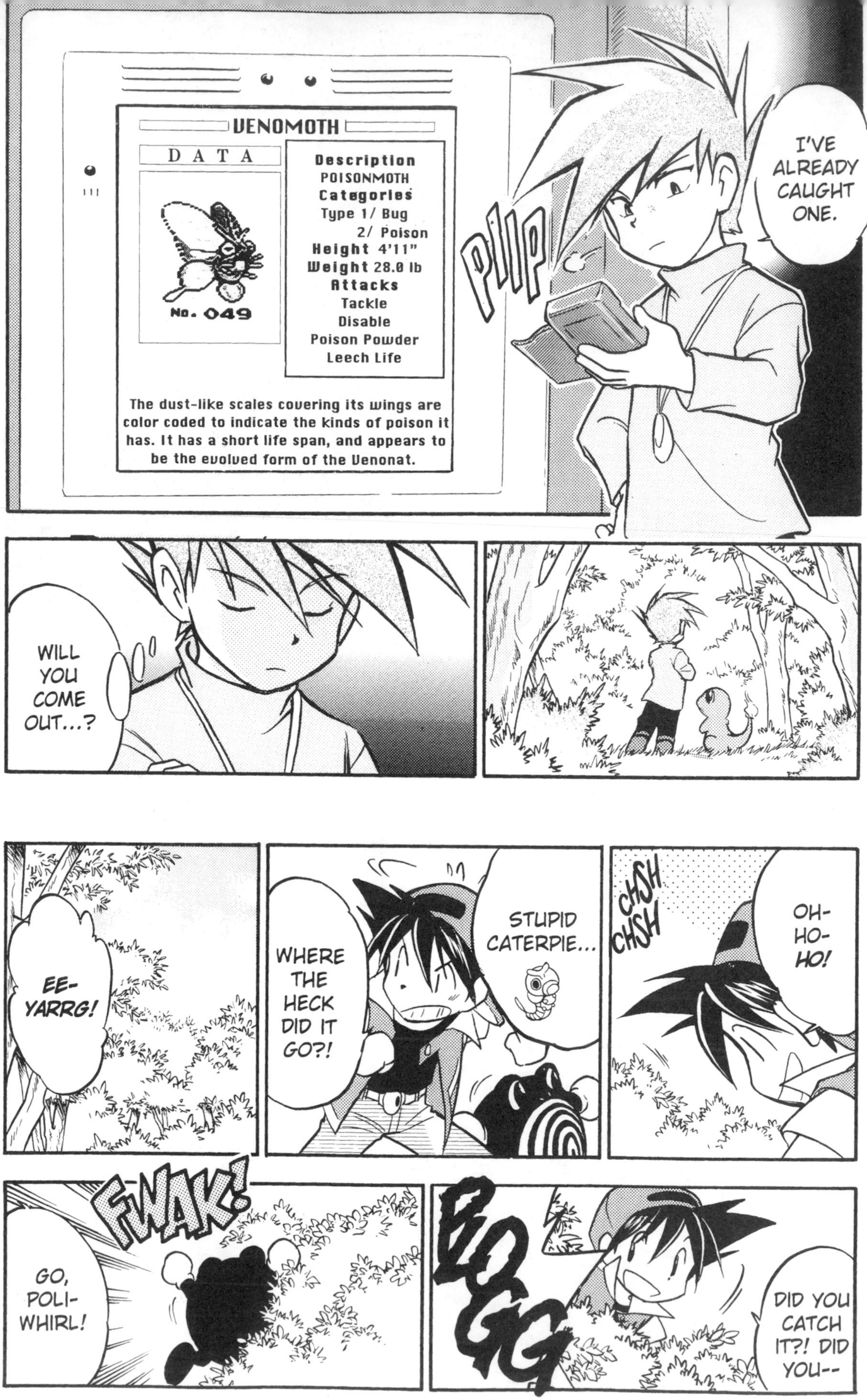
VENOMOTH
DATA
No. 049
Description
POISONMOTH
Categories
Type 1/ Bug
2/ Poison
Height 4'11"
Weight 28.0 lb
Attacks
Tackle
Disable
Poison Powder
Leech Life
The dust-like scales covering its wings are color coded to indicate the kinds of poison it has. It has a short life span, and appears to be the evolved form of the Venonat.
PLIP
I'VE ALREADY CAUGHT ONE.
WILL YOU COME OUT...?
EE-YARRG!
WHERE THE HECK DID IT GO?!
STUPID CATERPIE...
CHSH CHSH
OH-HO-HO!
FWAK!
GO, POLI-WHIRL!
BLOGG
DID YOU CATCH IT?! DID YOU--

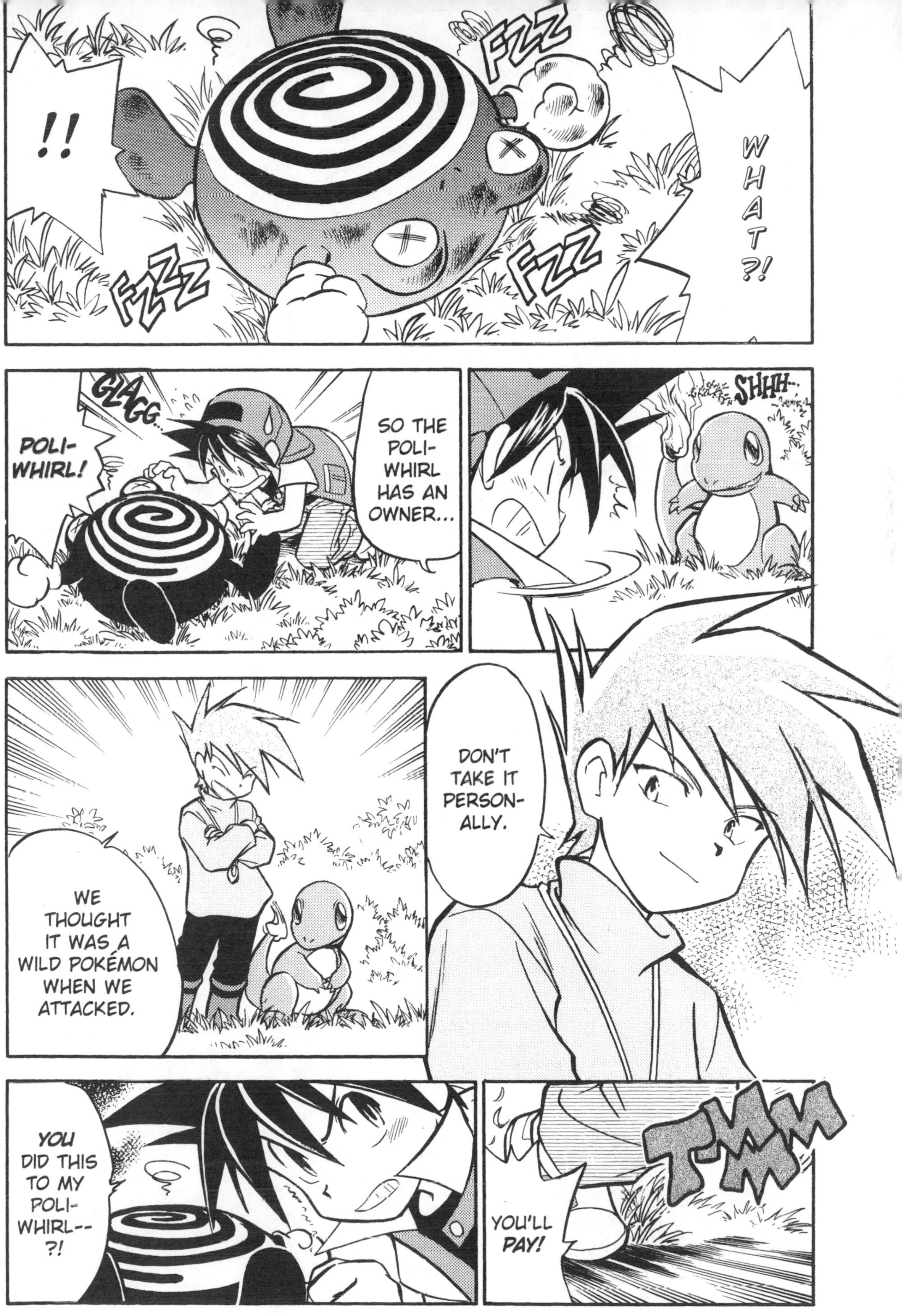
!!
FZZZ
FZZ
FZZ
WHAT?!
GLAGG...
POLI-WHIRL!
SO THE POLI-WHIRL HAS AN OWNER...
SHHH...
WE THOUGHT IT WAS A WILD POKÉMON WHEN WE ATTACKED.
DON'T TAKE IT PERSON-ALLY.
YOU DID THIS TO MY POLI-WHIRL--?!
T-MMM
YOU'LL PAY!

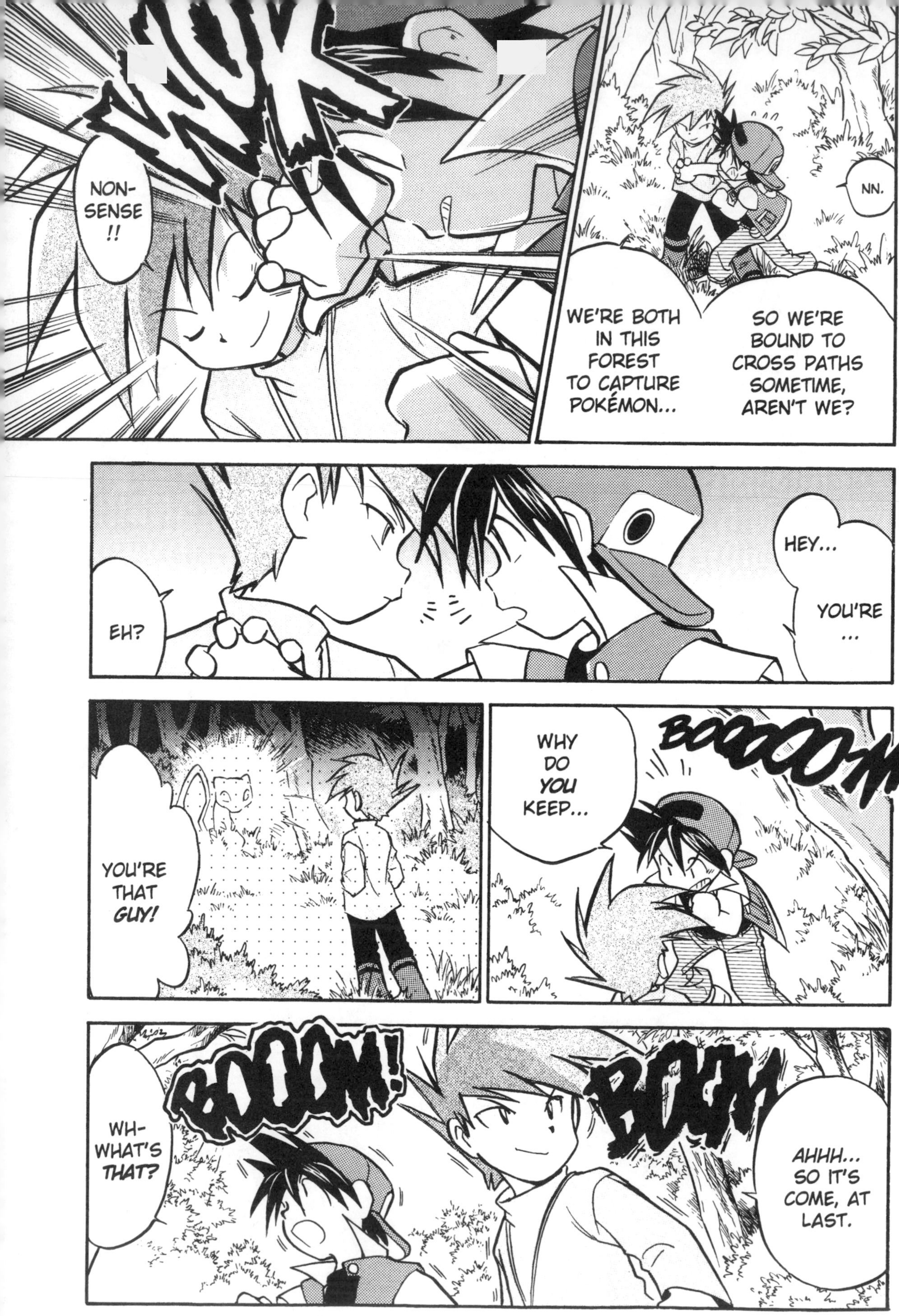
NON-SENSE!!
NN.
WE'RE BOTH IN THIS FOREST TO CAPTURE POKÉMON...
SO WE'RE BOUND TO CROSS PATHS SOMETIME, AREN'T WE?
EH?
HEY...
YOU'RE ...
YOU'RE THAT GUY!
WHY DO YOU KEEP...
BOOOOOOM
WH-WHAT'S THAT?
BOOOM!
BOOM
AHHH... SO IT'S COME, AT LAST.

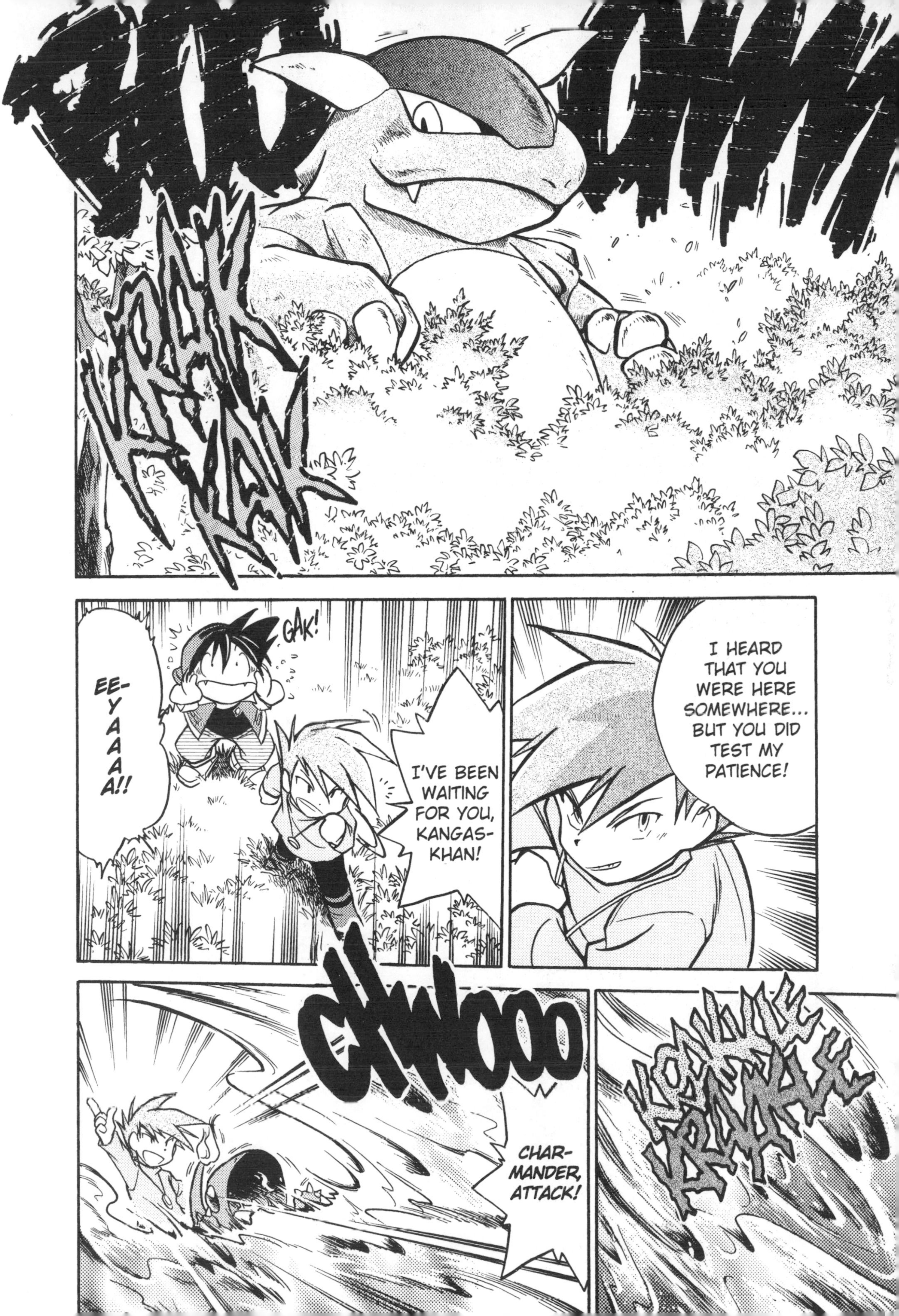
GAK!
EE-YAAAAAA!!
I'VE BEEN WAITING FOR YOU, KANGAS-KHAN!
I HEARD THAT YOU WERE HERE SOMEWHERE... BUT YOU DID TEST MY PATIENCE!
CHWOOO
CHAR-MANDER, ATTACK!

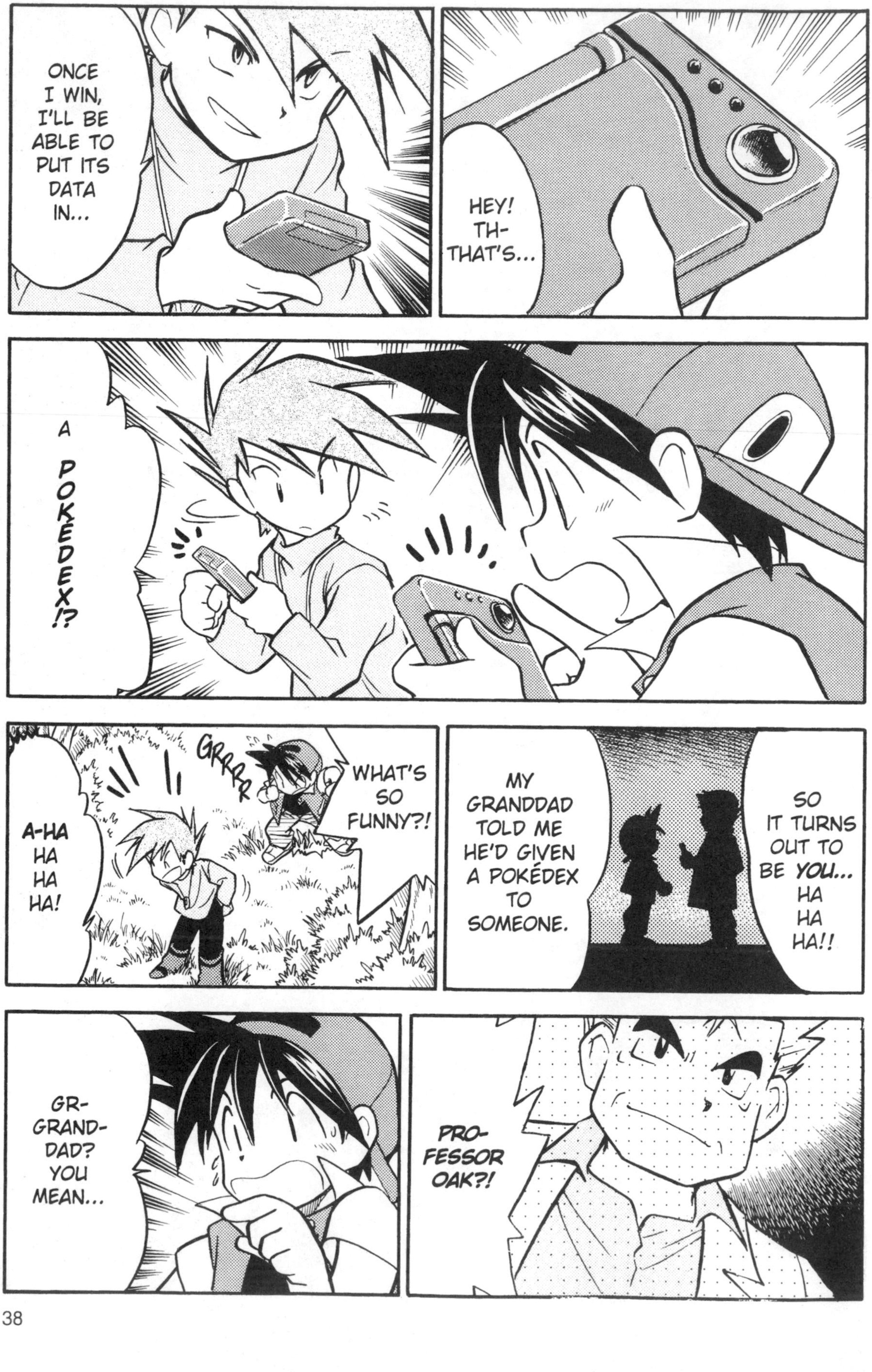
ONCE I WIN, I'LL BE ABLE TO PUT ITS DATA IN...
HEY! TH-THAT'S...
A POKÉDEX!?
A-HA HA HA HA!
GRRRR
WHAT'S SO FUNNY?!
MY GRANDDAD TOLD ME HE'D GIVEN A POKÉDEX TO SOMEONE.
SO IT TURNS OUT TO BE YOU... HA HA HA!!
GR-GRAND-DAD? YOU MEAN...
PRO-FESSOR OAK?!

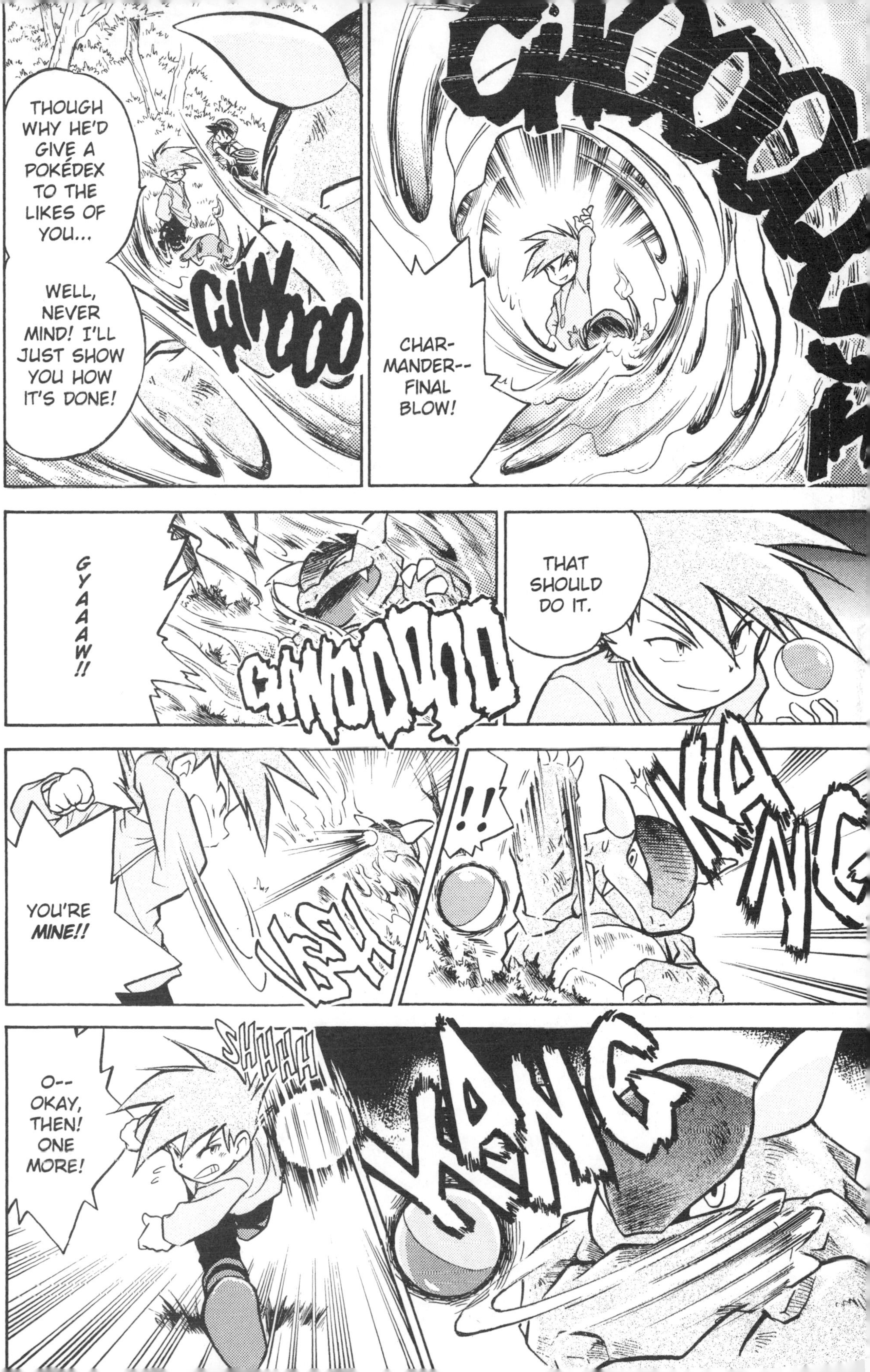
THOUGH WHY HE'D GIVE A POKÉDEX TO THE LIKES OF YOU...
WELL, NEVER MIND! I'LL JUST SHOW YOU HOW IT'S DONE!
CHAR-MANDER--FINAL BLOW!
GYAAAAW!!
THAT SHOULD DO IT.
YOU'RE MINE!!
!!
KANG
O--OKAY, THEN! ONE MORE!
SHHHH
KANG

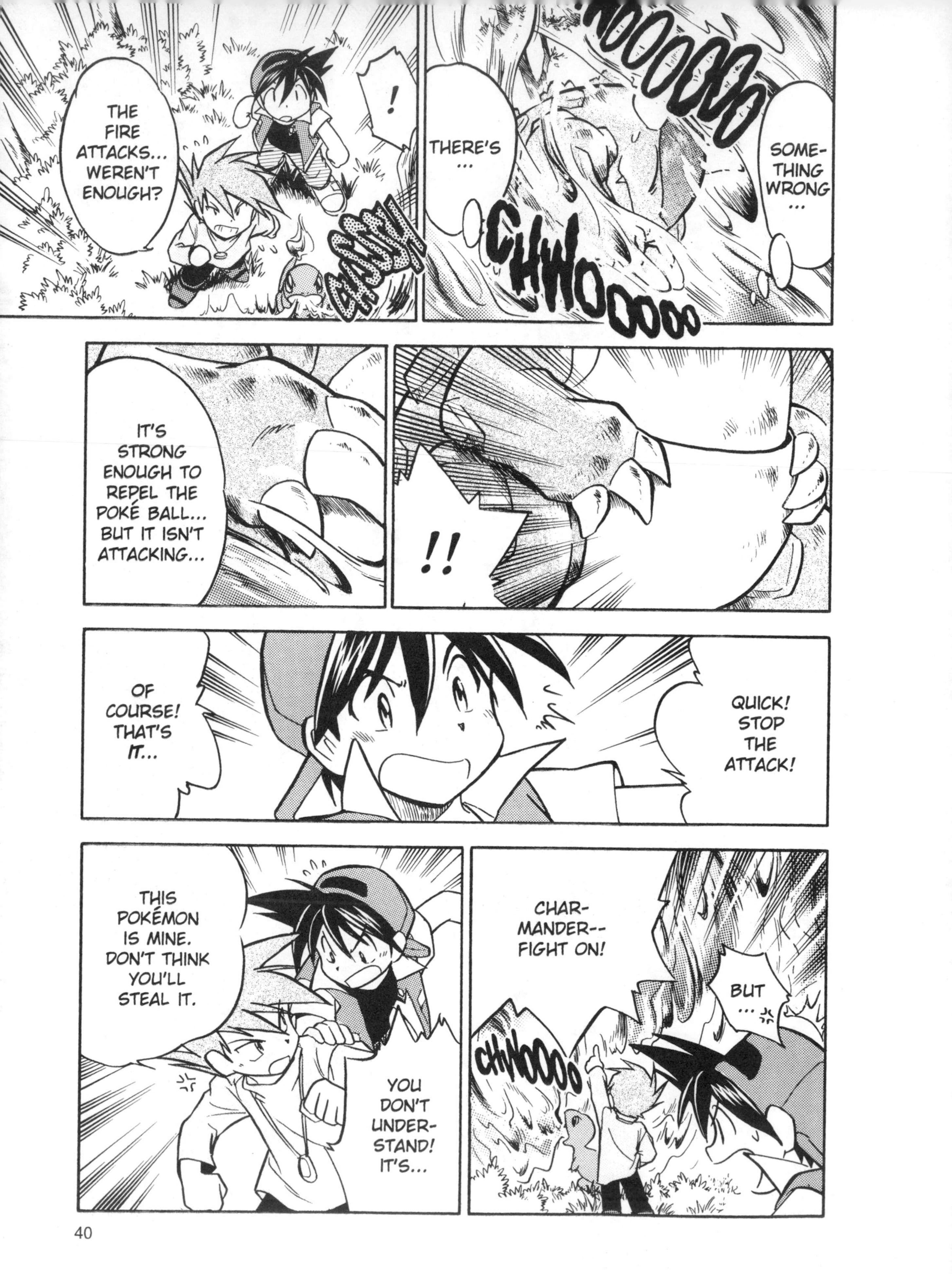
THE FIRE ATTACKS... WEREN'T ENOUGH?
!
THERE'S ...
SOME-THING WRONG ...
CHWOOOOO
IT'S STRONG ENOUGH TO REPEL THE POKÉ BALL... BUT IT ISN'T ATTACKING...
!!
OF COURSE! THAT'S IT...
QUICK! STOP THE ATTACK!
THIS POKÉMON IS MINE. DON'T THINK YOU'LL STEAL IT.
YOU DON'T UNDER-STAND! IT'S...
CHAR-MANDER--FIGHT ON!
BUT ...
CHWOOOO

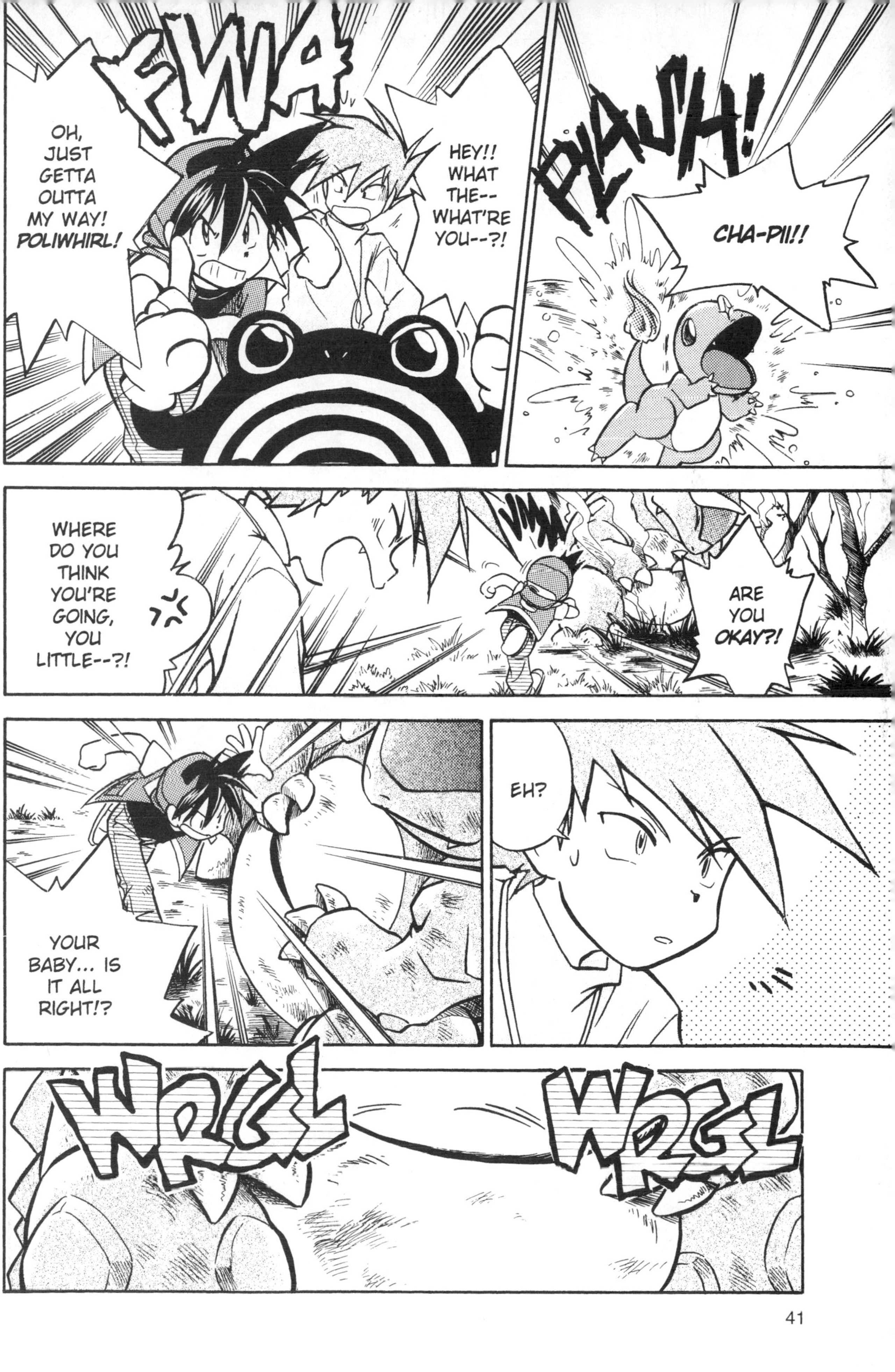
FWA
OH, JUST GETTA OUTTA MY WAY! POLIWHIRL!
HEY!! WHAT THE-- WHAT'RE YOU--?!
PLASH!
CHA-PII!!
WHERE DO YOU THINK YOU'RE GOING, YOU LITTLE--?!
ARE YOU OKAY?!
YOUR BABY... IS IT ALL RIGHT!?
EH?
WRGL
WRGL

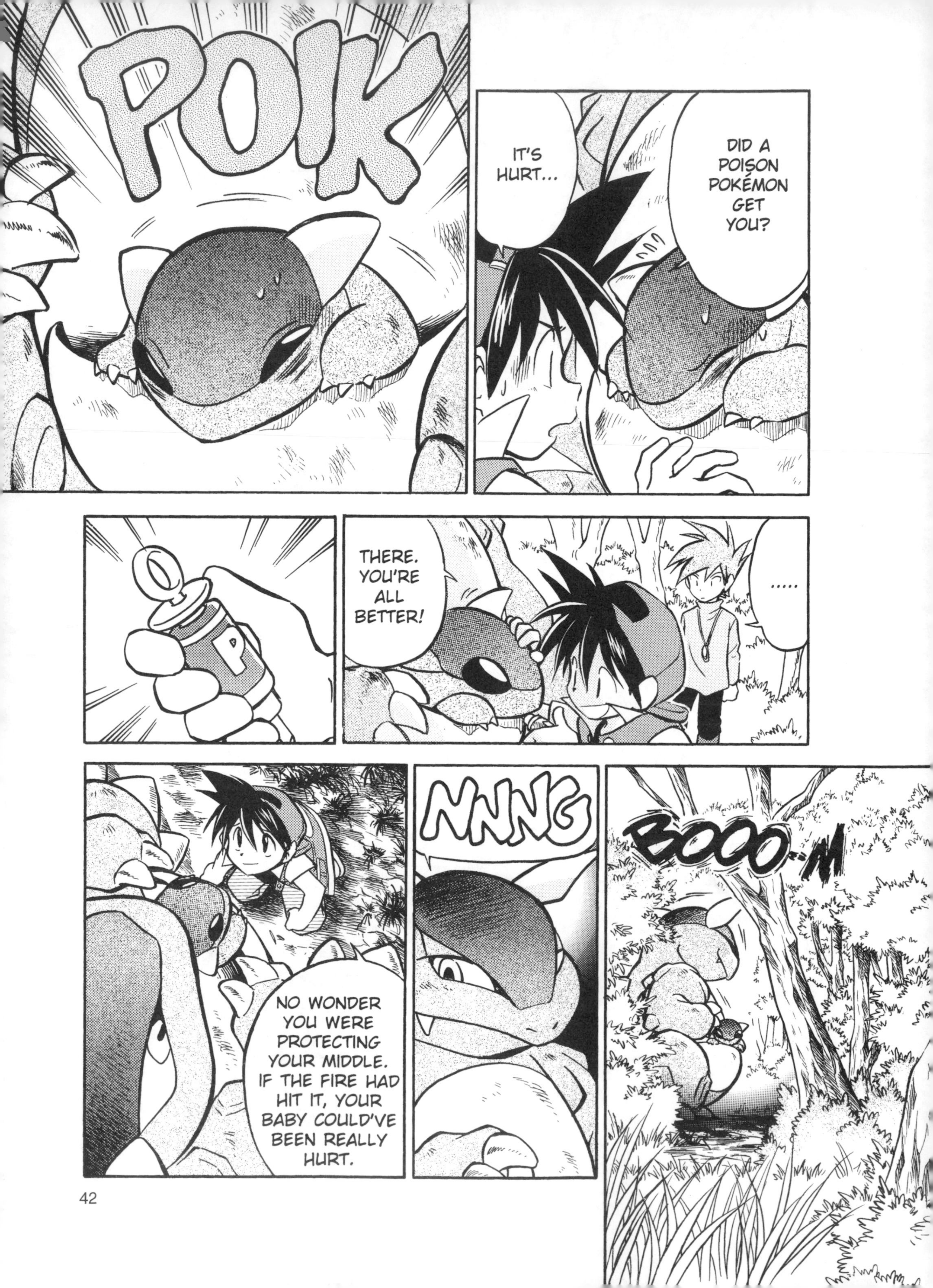
POK
IT'S HURT...
DID A POISON POKÉMON GET YOU?
THERE. YOU'RE ALL BETTER!
.....
NO WONDER YOU WERE PROTECTING YOUR MIDDLE. IF THE FIRE HAD HIT IT, YOUR BABY COULD'VE BEEN REALLY HURT.
NNNG
BOOOM

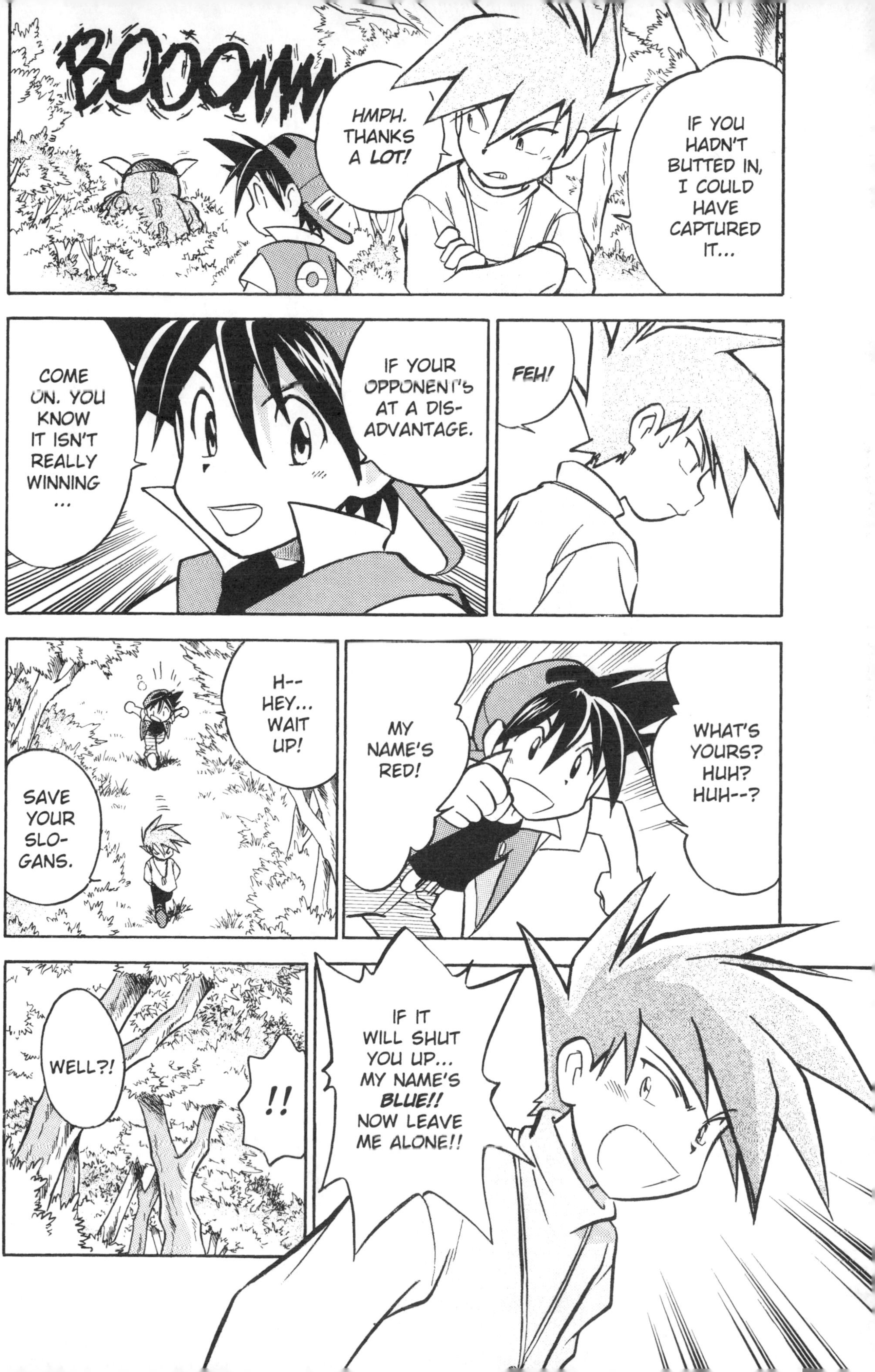
BOOOM
HMPH. THANKS A LOT!
IF YOU HADN'T BUTTED IN, I COULD HAVE CAPTURED IT...
COME ON. YOU KNOW IT ISN'T REALLY WINNING...
IF YOUR OPPONENT'S AT A DIS-ADVANTAGE.
FEH!
SAVE YOUR SLO-GANS.
H-- HEY... WAIT UP!
MY NAME'S RED!
WHAT'S YOURS? HUH? HUH--?
WELL?!
!!
IF IT WILL SHUT YOU UP... MY NAME'S BLUE!! NOW LEAVE ME ALONE!!

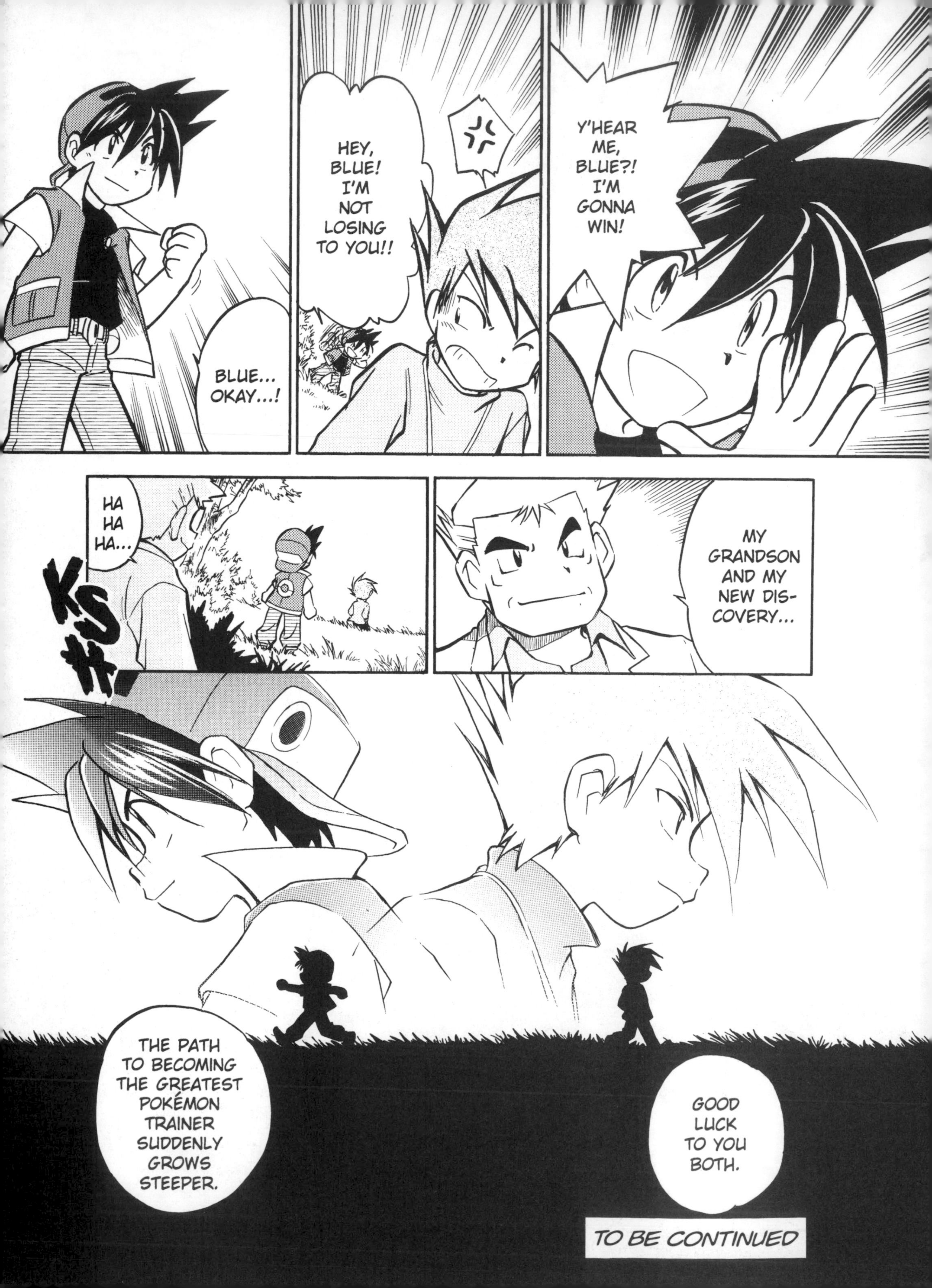
BLUE... OKAY...!
HEY, BLUE! I'M NOT LOSING TO YOU!!
Y'HEAR ME, BLUE?! I'M GONNA WIN!
HA HA HA...
KSSH
MY GRANDSON AND MY NEW DIS-COVERY...
THE PATH TO BECOMING THE GREATEST POKÉMON TRAINER SUDDENLY GROWS STEEPER.
GOOD LUCK TO YOU BOTH.
TO BE CONTINUED

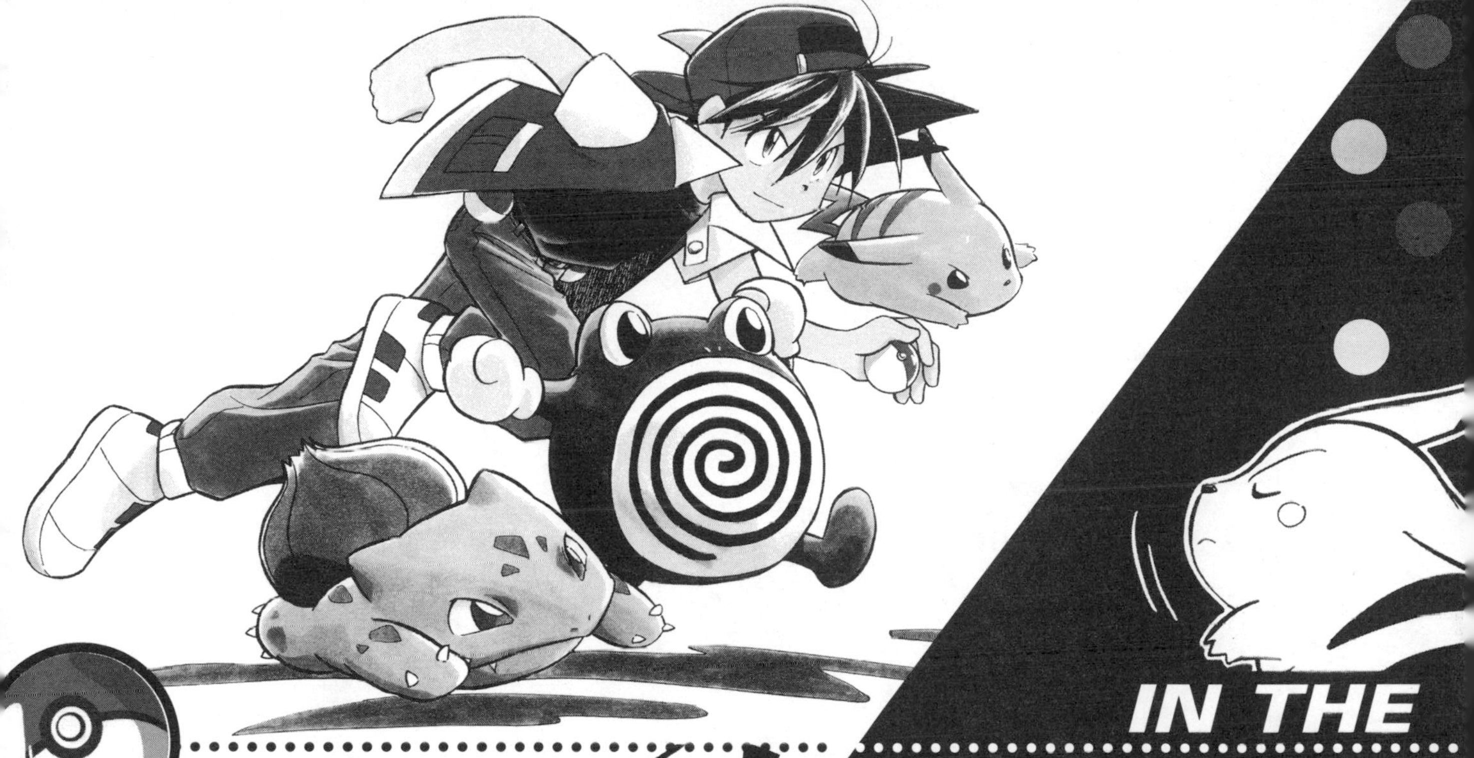

IN THE NEXT ISSUE:

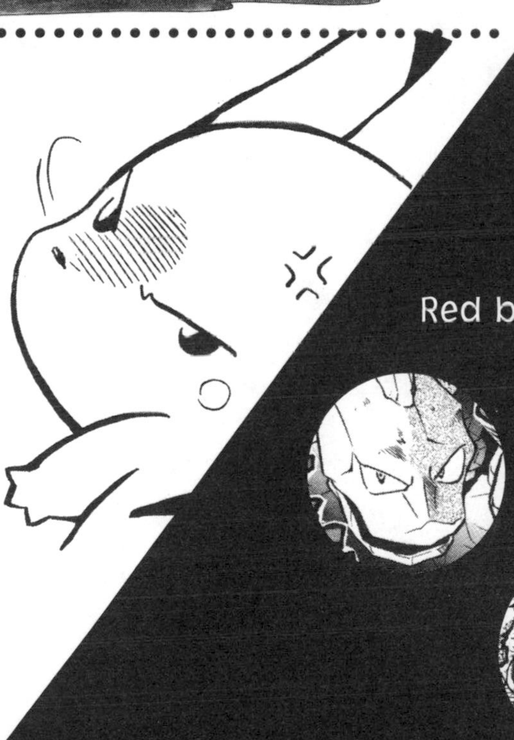

Pikachu is public enemy number one!

Red battles in the tournament at Pewter City Gym for the Boulder Badge!

Pikachu Vs. Onix!!

Gyarados is on the rampage!

Misty and Red team up!

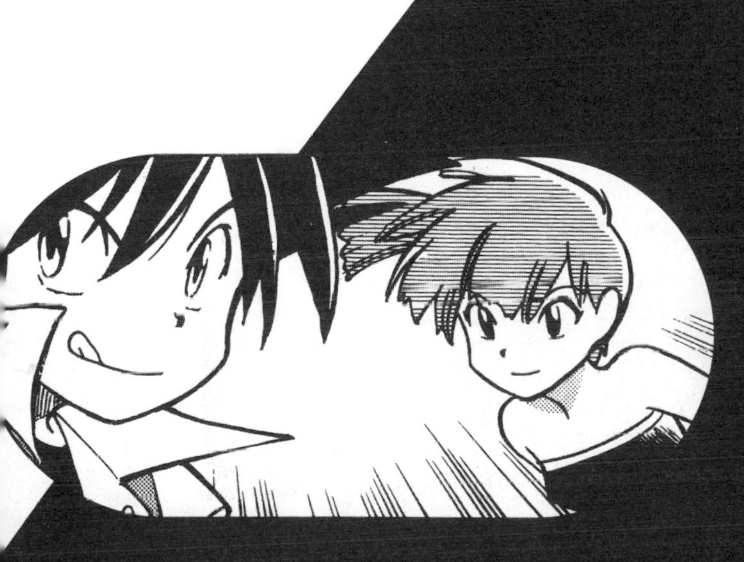

Get the next exciting issue:
Wanted: Pikachu
on sale soon!

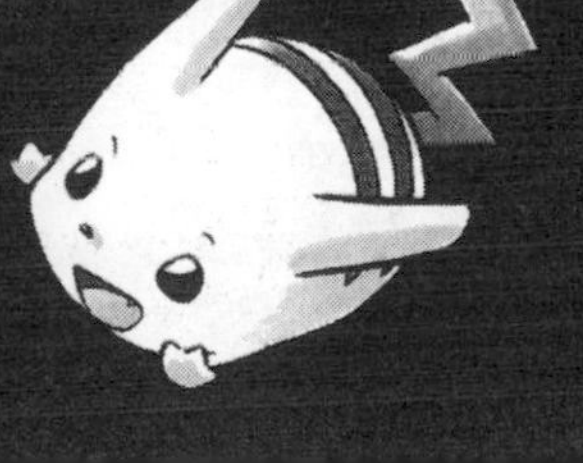

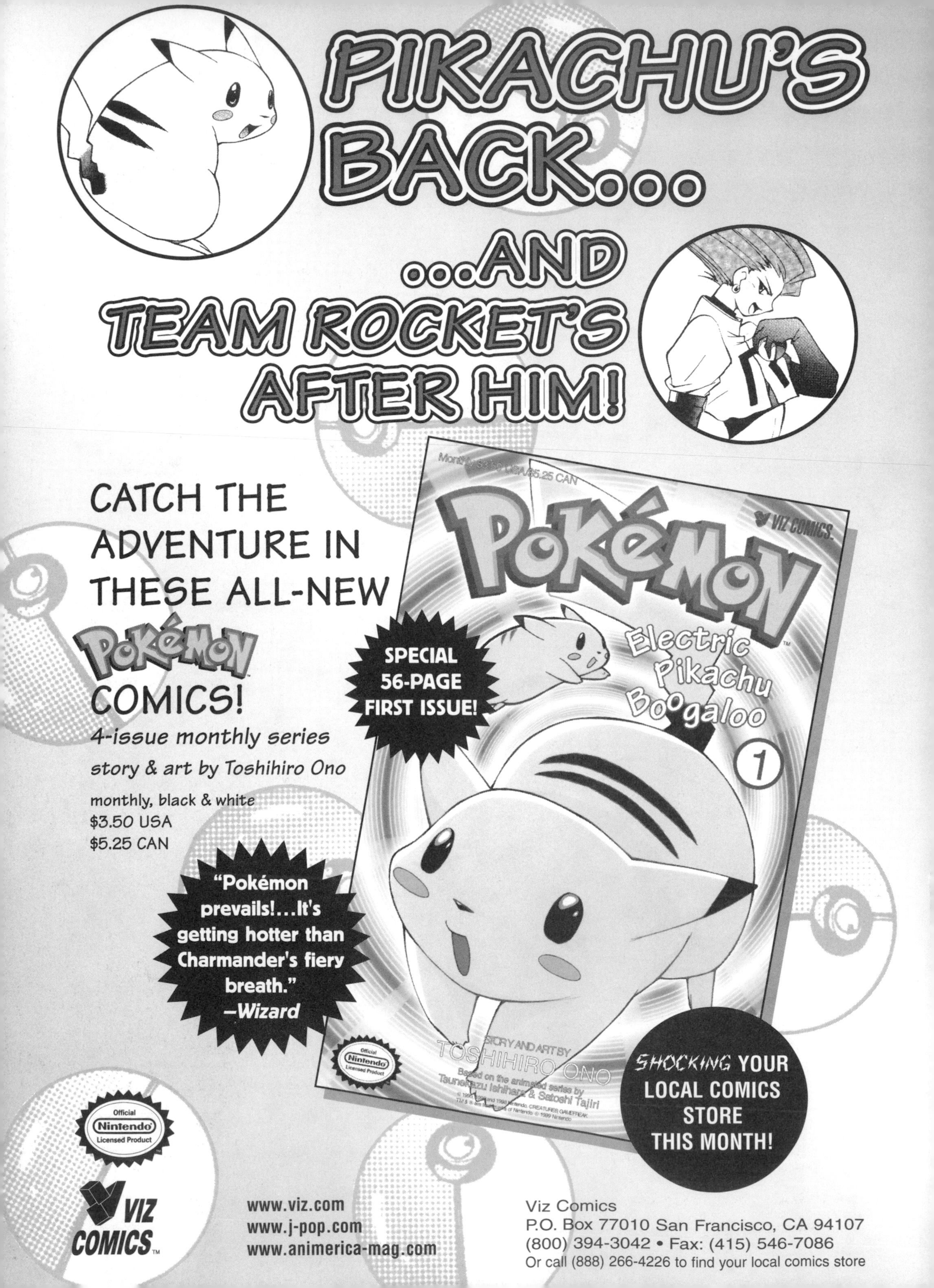

PIKACHU'S BACK...
...AND TEAM ROCKET'S AFTER HIM!
CATCH THE ADVENTURE IN THESE ALL-NEW
POKÉMON
COMICS!
4-issue monthly series
story & art by Toshihiro Ono
monthly, black & white
$3.50 USA
$5.25 CAN
VIZ COMICS.
POKÉMON
Electric Pikachu Boogaloo
1
SPECIAL 56-PAGE FIRST ISSUE!
"Pokémon prevails!...It's getting hotter than Charmander's fiery breath." —Wizard
STORY AND ART BY TOSHIHIRO ONO
Official Nintendo Licensed Product
SHOCKING YOUR LOCAL COMICS STORE THIS MONTH!
Official Nintendo Licensed Product
VIZ COMICS
www.viz.com
www.j-pop.com
www.animerica-mag.com
Viz Comics
P.O. Box 77010 San Francisco, CA 94107
(800) 394-3042 • Fax: (415) 546-7086
Or call (888) 266-4226 to find your local comics store

The story of a boy who turns into a girl, a father who turns into a panda, and the weird Chinese curse that did it to 'em!

Rumiko Takahashi's
Ranma ½™

Ranma 1/2 ©1999 Rumiko Takahashi/Shogakukan, Inc.

Videos!

Four seasons of the anime TV series, plus movies and original animated videos. Available in English or in Japanese with English subtitles.

TITLE	ENGLISH	SUBTITLED
Original TV Series (Vols. 1-9)	$29.95 ea.	n/a
Collector's Edition TV Series (Vols. 1-6)	n/a	$34.95 ea.
Anything-Goes Martial Arts (Vols. 1-11)	$24.95 ea.	$29.95 ea.
Hard Battle (Vols. 1-12)	$24.95 ea.	$29.95 ea.
Outta Control (Vols. 1-12)	$24.95 ea.	Coming Soon
OAVs Vols. 1-6 (Vols. 1-3 are English-only)	$29.95 ea.	$29.95 ea.
Collector's Editions OAVs (Vols. 1-2)	n/a	$34.95 ea.
Video Jukebox	n/a	$14.95 ea.
Movie: Big Trouble in Nekonron, China	$34.95 ea.	$34.95 ea.
2nd Movie: Nihao My Concubine	$34.95 ea.	$34.95 ea.
Digital Dojo Box Set (9 Vols.)	$199.95 ea.	n/a
Anything-Goes Box Set (11 Vols.)	$199.95 ea.	n/a
OAV Box Set (6 Vols.)	$124.95 ea.	n/a
Hard Battle Box Set (12 Vols.)	$199.95 ea.	n/a

Plus!

Graphic Novels: 13 volumes & counting!

T-Shirts: 7 styles available in different sizes!

Music: 6 soundtracks from the anime TV series and movies.

Monthly Comics: Available by subscription or individual issues!

Merchandise: Baseball caps, Cappuccino mugs, watches, postcards & more!